MW01504302

The Hunt

by
David Francis

authorHOUSE®

AuthorHouse™
1663 Liberty Drive
Bloomington, IN 47403
www.authorhouse.com
Phone: 1-800-839-8640

First published by AuthorHouse 4/5/2011

ISBN: 978-1-4520-1233-9 (e)
ISBN: 978-1-4520-1231-5 (sc)

Library of Congress Control Number: 2010913646

Printed in the United States of America

This book is printed on acid-free paper.

To my wife Ronél for her encouragement in writing this book. All my love.

*Mom and Dad, Thank you for introducing me
to the beauty of nature and the gift of family*

Dedicated to Tokkie & the late Johan Ströh

Cover Illustration by Wendy Rottner

Wendy, Many thanks for your time and dedication in bringing "The King" to life.

Prologue

When the fall comes, think of me. I can be heard on any mountain, seen in any town, and felt in any man who has a passion for living as his father lived, learning what he taught, and breathing the free crisp autumn air that he breathed. And so I climb the high mountain in search of the great buck, if only to get a glimpse of him and feel my heart skip a beat before it jumps out of my chest. The great buck I seek is king and keeper of the woods, just as I am the keeper of all that my father taught. And as I do all that I can to bring the great beast to my sight, I know that he is king and that it is I who am wounded, for time is fleeting, and my family is gone. The king is proud and runs hard with great, outstretched strides that make him invisible between the trees. His loins have succeeded in carrying a bloodline of superiority to a land that will prosper whether he now lives or dies. But I will surely die ….

Chapter 1

THE BRITTANY WOKE the old man early. It was a chilly October morning. The first frost of the season had settled in on the valley. Elmer was already half-awake. It was hard for him to sleep. When the weather changed he grew restless. The arthritis made sleeping difficult. The arthritis made a lot of things difficult. He sat up in bed and switched on the lamp sitting on the nightstand. A mirror across the floor resting on a dresser took in the figure on the bed. Two crease marks from a pillow ran down a scruffy face. A thin tuft of hair stuck up awkwardly off a lonely bald top. Deep-set eyes squinted under bushy salt and pepper eyebrows. He set his eyes on the mirror, and the eyes in the mirror looked back. The eyes in the mirror were frequent guests early in the morning, but that was about the only time they met. The old man had no faith in the mirror and little reason to care for the increasingly unfamiliar site that gazed awkwardly back at him. Turning to the clock on the nightstand, he waited for the little hand to come into focus, and then sighed when it eventually did.

"Only quarter after five, Bo. You usually make it till at least quarter to six."

He rubbed thick fingers and a calloused hand, swollen

at the joints, back and forth over the tuft of hair while he collected his thoughts.

"Well, I guess we're both getting old. Can't hold it in like we used to."

He folded the covers back and hung a pair of pale white feet, long and bony, over the edge of the bed. Daybreak had yet to poke through the windows. The room was cold. He conveniently fell into a ratty pair of corduroy slippers when his feet met the floor. Wearing a pair of long johns and slightly bent at the back and knees, master and servant slowly marched out the room and down the hall to the kitchen door. The old man's bones cracked as the dog's nails clicked on the wooden floor that creaked under their weight. Together they played as an orchestra of the aged. The Brittany got to the door first and sat patiently with a stiff closed muzzle and serious eyes that followed the old man to the door and watched him fuss with the black iron latch. He pulled open the door and pushed open the weathered, rickety white-framed screen.

"Go on, Bo."

He looked down at his old dog, which sat still and stared up earnestly at the old man. He was a nine-year-old Brittany spaniel, with white fur and rust-colored patches about the face and body. He may have been older. Elmer had to guess his age.

Five years earlier, only days after Elmer's wife Violet was put in the ground, the dog appeared at his door. He was a mangy looking animal with matted fur and burs knotted about the neck and ears. He smelled worse than a dead snake and with ribs slightly exposed under the matted fur, looked like he was well on his way to becoming a corpse of the undead. The old man cast him out, although he felt bad. His grieving heart had no time to care for a sick, wandering pup, he thought. But the dog would not leave. One morning while chopping some wood in the field behind the house, he saw the dog running around half-crazed in the woods. When Elmer went to investigate, he found the Brittany frozen, his nose pointing to the base of a fallen hickory tree that lay rotted and forgotten. As the old man approached, a rabbit darted out from under the tree as if its fluffy white tail was on fire. The dog didn't run after but instead turned and stared back at the old man intently, as if to say, "Why didn't you shoot?"

The two stared at one another. A connection was made. The dog had obviously made a living on hunting whatever he could find, but for how long the old man couldn't figure.

"Well, I guess I ruined your breakfast. Come on with me back to the house and I'll get ya something from the cupboard. May not be as good as fresh rabbit, though."

The Brittany followed the old man back to the house. The old man disappeared inside, and the dog patiently waited on the porch. When he returned it was with a plate of leftover stew. He placed it on the porch.

"Here ya go, boy. I think this might satisfy you for a little while."

The old man believed in providence. Sure, it could have been just a dumb coincidence that this sick and lonely pup came into his yard only days after Violet's death, but the old man didn't think so. Violet, he believed, guided this poor homeless creature to him. She knew how lonely he would be without her. *She always knew*, he thought.

He watched intently with folded arms as the hungry dog licked the plate clean.

"You came to me homeless and beggin' for food, and I cast you out. You came to me like an ol' bohemian!"

Bo, as this wandering creature came to be called, had found a home, and the old man had found a friend and hunting partner.

Bo continued to sit stone-faced and frozen as Elmer peered out the kitchen door. The night was giving over ever grudgingly to the morning. The pumpkins on the porch were frosted over. He took one last look back at his old companion, but still the Brittany would not move.

"I don't know what your problem is."

He flicked the kitchen light switch to the right of the door and sat at the table. Again he rubbed his hand back and forth over his bald head and thought for a moment.

"Ol' Bohemian, you got that urge, don't you. Why you been acting like this all week. I know what your problem is. You're telling me it's time to do some hunting. Old dogs like you and I always get that urge with the weather change. Well, I think you're probably right, and I'll agree with you more if we can find some birds to hunt. I don't know why you gotta wake me this early ta tell me though. That's not right!"

Bo stared back at the old man intently with excited brown eyes and a head slightly cocked to one side. His nails slid on the kitchen floor, and he had to readjust his footing every now and again. But aside from that, his stare was intense and unbroken.

"Well, let me get my clothes on and get some breakfast. Ol' Bo, you haven't let me down in all the years I known ya! I still wish ya wouldn't wake me so early though. Maybe we'll go over ta Jenkins' farm and wake him up."

The old man walked on down the hall back to the bedroom to make ready for the day.

Chapter 2

THE OLD MAN opened the door of his pickup, and the
Brittany jumped up onto the seat. His master followed
him in and cranked up the cold engine. They drove south
down Clinton Corners Farm Road and at the fork veered
left onto Pancake Hollow. It was less than a four mile
journey, and the old man knew it all too well. The road
was narrow and uneven with a high bow in the middle.
The road was filled with potholes and the old man knew
every one of them, zigzagging the truck this way and
that. Much of the road had nothing more than remnants
of pavement. Up a rise and slight bend in the road and
over a one-lane iron bridge the truck putted along. The
land opened up with fields on either side. The road graded
upward jagged and quick, and without warning appeared
the driveway of the Jenkins Homestead and the apple
farm behind it. Sprawling hills of trees bearing luscious,
deep red fruit rose aptly up a grand hill and a formidable
mountain loomed large behind it.

Now, the old man loved to hunt, and in his younger
years was well known throughout the county as a darn
good hunter and tracker. He learned how to hunt from
his father, who considered it, as many do, a rite of passage
from boy to young man. The old man could recall

countless hunts and expeditions with his father and brothers and the big deer that ran the hills of Jenkins Mountain, or as should be said, were stopped from running those great hills. But now he was old, and his legs could not climb so well, and his hands would ache from carrying the heavy rifle for so many hours on cold November days. For this reason and others, the old man reserved much of his attention for hunting grouse during the fall months with his trusty companion Bo, although the urge to go after the big game nudged him this way and that every so often.

Elmer parked the truck in the usual spot, a small section of yard to which he gave little consideration and to which Bo usually gave even less. This spot was to the right of the driveway and directly under the fully extended branches of a two-hundred–year-old maple tree. The tree was at its peak color, and upon getting out of the truck, the old man took a moment and gazed in amazement at the majestic site before him. The moment was of course interrupted by Bo, who cocked a leg to its base; this being the common ritual of a man and his dog.

Jenkins' farmhouse was just on the other side of the driveway. It was a white stone house that dated back before the American Revolution. Abraham Jenkins, the patriarch of the apple farm, was fond of telling stories of how his great-grandfather, five generations removed, gave food and shelter to patriot troops who passed through one winter. Elmer had heard the story many times, but some of the details were a tad shade of gray, possibly from Abe Jenkins' own literary license for detail and the blurriness created between fact, fiction, and storytelling. But the old man took solace in the one clear fact that everything does get better with the retelling. The farm had a past, and that was the important thing, and so did this mountain. For Elmer this would always be true.

Pulling his gun from the truck, the old man broke open the barrels and blew into them, giving them a quick cleaning.

"C'mon, Bo. Let's go."

They walked up a dirt driveway that was just to the right of the old farmhouse, until the driveway turned into a dirt tractor road. It was muddy and rocky. From many years of use from horses to heavy wagons and tractors, the road had sunken in some areas. They followed the road to a small wooden bridge. Big, thick wooden beams, about thirty of them lying side by side, made up the bridge and were barely distinguishable because the land had seemed to swallow them. In fact, the bridge wouldn't have been noticed at all if not for the ends that stuck straight out and of course the pancake hollow brook that ran underneath it.

Bo took the lead and trotted over the bridge, and the old man followed. On the other side of the brook and to the left of the dirt road was a barn. It was a wooden barn in need of much repair. A rusted tin roof sat upon heavy creosote beams and both were supported by a stone foundation built about the same period as the farmhouse. It was a rundown old barn that looked more like a shack than a barn, but it had sheltered everything from soldiers to plow horses, wagons to tractors, and smelled of hay, creosote, horse manure, and rotten apples. The road winded its way up a small hill and around to the other side of the barn where in a corral stood a handsome gray plow horse. Upon seeing the old man and the Brittany, the horse slowly meandered out to the fence line to investigate, each hoof carelessly pounding into its muddy domain. The old man pulled an apple out of his hunting coat and held it out between the fence posts. The horse consumed the whole apple in one bite, shoving its massive cold snout into the man's hand. The old man ran his hand up and down the long white mane from its forehead to its snout.

"Hey, Ol' Gray, have you seen any birds, huh? Any birds out here this morning?"

The horse gave a low, guttural whinny and flipped its long, shaggy tail, showing its gratitude for the attention.

Man and dog continued on, walking the dirt road until it turned into more of a trail than a road, as the grass had grown over much of it, leaving just a rut of muddy tire tracks on either side. It twisted and turned and ascended up the hill, splitting the north and south orchards of Jenkins farm. On each side of the trail was a stone wall covered in high grass and wild rose bushes. The wall acted as a cemetery for discarded machinery and equipment. There was an old, abandoned tractor and other assorted tools; a tire; a rusted out crow bar; a half-rotted wooden cart wagon; fifty or so wooden pallets; the rusted out carcass of a pickup truck, and some two dozen or so half-rotted apple crates that made up the graveyard of Jenkins' apple farm. The display was testament to over two hundred years of a working farm. Past each stone wall lay the four hundred acres of apple trees that encompassed Jenkins' property.

The two made their way up the great hill about a half-mile to the wood line of Jenkins Mountain and stopped at the point where the trail snaked into the woods. The old man was winded and needed a rest. He looked back at the hill he had climbed. Down in the valley was Jenkins' house and the massive spread of his farm. The sun had risen up over the mountain and shone bright, wishing the valley a good morning. The old man stood in the shade of the hill, pulled a handkerchief out of his hunting coat, and wiped the sweat from his forehead.

"I'm still in pretty good shape!" He rolled up the handkerchief slowly, giving him some time to catch his breath. He stuffed the handkerchief back into his coat. He took one last glance down at the fields and then disappeared into the woods.

Together the old man and the Brittany worked their way up through some cedars and to the first ledge of the mountain. On top of the first ledge was a large cluster of spruce trees and beyond that was a blowdown, a clearing in the woods where the trees were blown over by storms and strong winds. It created a nice hiding place for many small animals and birds, and it was here that Bo's keen instincts took over and the old man knew it. He watched carefully as Bo worked his way through the spruce, nose low to the ground, sniffing the earth for the scent of a grouse. Several times the dog went on point, moving slowly and looking carefully in through the branches, his nose getting lower and lower. The old man kept his Browning out in front, his finger gently resting on the trigger. Bo moved carefully, his paws touching down lightly, almost weightless on the leaves. The blowdown spread across a large area, and the cover was extremely thick with briars and bur patches. The Brittany worked his way through it, and the old man followed patiently but attentively a short distance away. The Brittany made his way through the thicket of brush when suddenly a rabbit darted through to the right of the dog. The man quickly raised his Browning and followed right, but was instantly drawn away by a thrashing raucous as three deer, a buck, and two does that were bedded down jumped up and took flight with great, powerful leaps over downed trees and brush. The brush shook and the branches crackled, breaking under the hoofs of the deer, as simultaneous flashes of tan and white moved against the green and gray backdrop of the blowdown. Shaking and dancing branches made all objects blend together in a fury of excitement that made the forest come alive. The dog out in front now, leaped and bit at the air as the man drew his Browning back to his left and crouched slightly, pulling it up to his shoulder, finger getting tighter on the trigger, bearing down just ahead of his trusty companion. Eyes wide now, a blur bursting up from the ground rocketing left, fanning wings, gun barrel out in front and squeeze into a thundering, booming echo as a fat ball of feathers torpedoed into a thicket of bramble. Leaves fluttered from the low leaning branches to the ground, sounding the death rattle. The forest breathed and then fell still and silent once again.

The old man's heart raced and with an unsteady hand he broke his gun open and pulled from the smoking barrel the empty casing. He reloaded and snapped the barrel closed as Bo forced his way through the brush to the downed bird. Carefully gripping the grouse in his mouth, the dog walked over to his master, who by this time was crouched on one knee awaiting his prize. The Brittany laid down to the left of the old man and dropped the bird at his paws, not wanting to give the bird over so quickly.

"Good job, Ol' Bo."

The old man pet the dog and scratched him under his chin and around his ears.

"Good boy, Ol' Bo. You did a great job. And I would have to say that I did a fine job as well, so how about that?"

With that he picked up the grouse and held it in his hands.

"This is a fine bird, Bo."

He looked down at the bird with an almost boyish smile filled with pride and accomplishment, and pet the bird with his heavy gloved hand so as to make neat again its ruffled feathers.

"Indeed, this is a fine bird."

With that he tucked the bird into the back pouch of his hunting coat.

Chapter 3

THAT EVENING, RESTING in his favorite lazy chair next to the fireplace, fire blazing amber, the hickory popping and sputtering as it burned, the old man thought about the day gone by. With a weathered writing journal on his lap, reading spectacles on his head, and sipping from a mug of hot coffee, the old man collected his thoughts and began to write with a dull pencil.

20th Oct. 1954. … Grouse shot with Browning
and Bo on Jenkins Hill, 1ˢᵗ ledge. Dog kicked
up two doe and buck at least 10pts.
Will think about going after?

The question mark said it all. He read it over one last time, and then closed the journal and placed it on the end table beside the lazy chair. The journal was old and matted with coffee stains on the cover. The pages were warped and wrinkled. The entries reflected more than fifty years of hunting and fishing, as well as thoughts on his life in the form of doodles and poems. One in particular had a special appeal, and he read it often, sometimes adding a line or two.

Driving down that country road past the open field
Once green fields filled with life that brings back days
gone by, days when we were young and spry ….

He took off his spectacles and gazed into the fire where the flames consumed all but the ends of the hickory log. It burned good and hot and the smell of burnt hickory filled the room.

The woods and the deer of Jenkins Mountain seemed to call to him as they always did. Upon seeing a buck in the fields or crossing the road, the man's temptation would grow and flow until his dreams of the great buck brought him back to his younger days.

In those years and they were many, he had quite a lot of luck on Jenkins Mountain. The deer would come down from the great hill and feed in the apple orchards from mid-summer through the fall when the rut began. The steady diet of apples and acorns that the mountain produced in abundance made the deer big and strong with glistening dark tan coats, and the bucks were of considerable size. It was not uncommon to see an eight- or ten-point buck on the lower ledges of the mountain in late summer and early fall. And those that were unfortunate enough to cross between the lower ledges of Jenkins Mountain and his orchards during hunting season usually wound up as trophies on a wall for a local hunter, or maybe the occasional hunter up from the city. And yes, there was also the occasional trespasser who decided to chance the will of Abraham Jenkins and hunt the great hill anyway. But Jenkins Mountain was one of a series of many. And there were many hills and many cornfields and apple orchards and swamps to hunt that Jenkins Mountain, and more importantly Jenkins himself, was not worth the burden if one wanted a nice simple hunt to bag a trophy. Elmer had taken his share of seven- and eight-point bucks from Jenkins Mountain, one of which peered out at him from the mantle above his fireplace.

One more time, he thought. *One more hunt on the big hill, back deep into the mountain between the ledges and post on the north side of the hill. That's where I'll find the big buck, even bigger than the one Bo jumped this morning.* The smart bucks, the old man knew, moved with diligence during the rut, and moved only under the cover of night between the swamp, the lower ledges, and the orchards. The hunters usually get the small and inexperienced ones that get caught out in the open just after daylight. But a big buck will feel safe deep in the heart of the mountain where most hunters would not care to go.

"The big one. Oh, how I want just one more chance at the big one," the old man proclaimed to the red hot embers.

Chapter 4

ONE EVENING IN late October, the old man visited a friend and former hunting pal Tony Canistro. At the kitchen table drinking espresso and eating Italian cookies that Tony's wife picked up at the local grocery, he recounted for Tony the time he had with Bo the week before. Tony leaned back on the kitchen chair, legs folded across one another. He was a big man and took up one full side of the table. Broad shouldered, his side paralleled the table and a massive dark-haired forearm rested on top of it, partially exposing a tattoo of an eagle and an American flag. As a young man his aim was deadly, and it had to be. Tony was a sharp shooter in the Marines in World War I and was decorated for saving two fellow marines who were trapped by the Germans. He still had the eyesight of a sharpshooter, although he could no longer hunt the mountains of his youth on account of bad knees. Tony still enjoyed hearing stories of hunting, and even more so to tell them. Over the years he depicted many stories of his great hunts. The stories took on a presence and an attitude of epic proportions, and some of them were actually true. They stood on their own. But the old man respected his accomplishments as a hunter and thought him to be the best shot he had ever seen.

Tony never missed, and for nearly forty years straight he never left the woods without venison to put in the freezer for his family, most of it being legal. Tony listened and smiled his wide-eyed, big-cheeked smile. He lavished in the old man's excitement of days past.

"It was quite a day for you, ahh," said Tony in a thick Italian accent.

"It sure was a fine day and the deer," the old man raised his hands above his head, mimicking that of a wide set of deer antlers. "They make me want to give it one last hunt for the big one."

"Eh! We're too old, you and I, to go climbing back in them hills. Our time is no more. We must leave it to the younger ones, ahh? You know what I do, I go to my son Johnny's, he's got the place on the other side of Eisgruber's farm, you know where I mean, and anyway I sit in a tree and pick 'em off as they come under."

He laughed as he spoke and motioned with his big, thick hands the act of pointing and shooting a rifle.

"I tell you every year you should come."

The old man would not hear of it.

"No offense, but if I'm going to hunt, I want to really hunt, use my senses, map out where the big one is, track him down, take aim and drag him down the hill, you know, the way we used to."

Although he had not wanted to offend his friend, it was obvious that he had. Tony's nostrils flared and his smile disappeared, leaving only the puffy, reddened cheeks and a cold, hard stare. His hands fell to the table like bricks. There was a brief silence, and then Tony bellowed in a sharp, clear voice,

"Old man, you are too old to hunt on them hills."

Tony folded his arms abruptly and sat back in his chair. Elmer just smiled, unwilling to let the words past his ears, unwilling to let common sense mix in with the thoughts that were in his mind.

Chapter 5

The deer play in the distance
Oh, won't they bring back the days gone by
Those days when we were young and spry ....

THE INDIAN SUMMER of October had gone and the old man took long walks with Bo up the long, rolling hills of Jenkins orchards. He walked as far as the lower ledges of the mountain up through the cedar and spruce, but each time was uneventful. Birds were scarce now and the deer had grown wary. The change of season made the big bucks ever more secretive and cunning, as if remembering the evils of the November previous, they made their way into hiding. But they could not cover their tracks that lined the trail along the lower ledges, nor were they intelligent enough to conceal their droppings or repel the temptation to rub their horns against saplings that lined the trail.

Upon examining one rub on a young maple tree, the old man could only fantasize as to the size of the buck that lashed out such punishment. Several of the lower branches were snapped clean off, and the tree's thin bark was shredded and lay in heaps around its base. The rub was a foot and a half in length and wrapped three-quarters of the way around the shaft of the maple, which measured about five-and-a-half inches in diameter. The horns had depressed the hardwood making jagged grooves in the base of the tree. He felt the grooves, the wound of the tree still fresh and damp. The wood was sticky, the grooves deep, and the rub only hours old. The old man removed some of the shreds of bark that lay around the tree and grinned, as if unearthing some great clue. In the soft earth beneath the shavings was a set of prints the size of a grapefruit in diameter. The old man took out his pen-knife from his pant pocket and placed it in the print of one hoof. It fit in with a quarter inch to spare. Indeed the assault on the maple and the tracks in the earth was testament of a big deer. Standing up straight, the old man peered southwest through an opening along a logging trail that worked its way up through the second ledge that made up the lower half of Jenkins Mountain.

"Bo," he called.

The dog looked up at his master attentively.

"Out there is a big buck, probably a ten-pointer and two hundred pounds if there's an ounce of him, and he's a game deer, that's for sure."

The old man looked earnestly now at his Brittany and with a grin and fiery tongue boasted, "And so am I, and I'll be here on opening day!"

Chapter 6

The mountain streams flow again
They flood the brook that meanders through the field
Cold crisp mountain air says good morning to the valley
The deer jump and play in the meadow
The field becomes green again
The blue birds awaken it from its slumber …

AT **3:30** AM the alarm clock rang out. Bo, asleep in the hallway, was the first to awaken. His claws clicked on the hardwood floor as he got up, shaking his collar and scratching himself feverishly as he made his way into the bedroom to greet the old man, who by this time was rolling over in bed. The clock continued to ring as he reached out with one hand and felt for the lamp on the nightstand and turned it on. He sat up in bed and put on his glasses that were also on the nightstand. He picked up the clock, eyed the time, and turned off the ringer. The room fell quiet once again. These sounds signified the first day of deer season.

The old man got out of bed and walked out the room and down the hall to the kitchen with Bo trailing in hot pursuit. He flicked on the kitchen light and went over to the kitchen door, pushed down on the old black iron latch, pulled open the door, and pushed open the rickety screen.

"Out you go, Bo. I know it's early, but I'm sure you'll manage." With that he let the screen door slam shut and closed the kitchen door behind him and walked back to his room to get dressed.

Ten minutes later the old man was back in the kitchen all decked out in a thick pair of white heavy-duty, full-length long johns and a pair of knee-high gray wool socks with red stripes that ran horizontally along the top of the sock. Under this was a pair of knee-high tube socks.

"I'm not going to freeze today," the old man mumbled as he again opened the kitchen door to find Bo waiting patiently on the porch.

For breakfast, the old man made a feast that any hunter would be willing to trade a secret as to the whereabouts of a big buck for a seat and a plate at the breakfast table. Hot off the griddle came three fried eggs, an enormous portion of re-fried potatoes, two slabs of scrapple, and two-day-old flapjacks topped off with a hunk of butter fat and fresh maple syrup, the latter compliments of Abraham Jenkins. A hot cup of reheated black coffee that was only a day old complemented the meal and hastened the exit of sleep from the old man's body.

After breakfast the old man put on his hunting clothes. In the den, draped over the lazy chair next to the fireplace, was the old man's red wool hunting pants complete with black suspenders, which he slipped on over his long johns. He tucked each pant leg into the wool socks so that the socks were on the outside of the bottoms of the pants, and he pulled them up as high as they could be pulled. Next to the fireplace was a weathered pair of hunting boots that the old man carefully laced up, crossing each lace and latching it to the lace hooks on either side of the upper of the boots. The uppers rose to just under the knee cap, and the man tied the laces off at the very top and then rolled down the red striped portion of the wool socks over the tops of the boots so as not to allow snow or water in through the top of the boots. A red wool coat lay over the back of the chair, and after putting it on and buttoning it up, he wrapped a thick, black gun belt around his waist and over the coat and buckled it tight. When his wife was alive she would make fun of his outfit, telling him he looked like a slimmer version of Santa Claus without the beard.

The old man thought of Violet whenever he put on his hunting clothes. It had been a long time; not a long time since thinking about her, 'cause he did everyday, but of putting on these clothes and thinking of the fun she would make of him. She used to get up with him and make him breakfast and coffee while he got dressed, and they would sit at the table together and talk while he ate his breakfast, her with a mug of hot coffee between her hands. She enjoyed the quiet of the morning; enjoyed getting up with him, seeing him off, kissing him goodbye and wishing him good luck.

"Bring us back some dinner, Santa," she would always say as she saw him to the kitchen door.

It's too quiet without her, he thought. As if almost sensing the old man's need, the Brittany rose from his place on the floor and lazily walked over to him, his toenails clicking on the hardwood floor. He looked upon the old man as if consoling him, as if that was possible for a dog to do. The old man bent down and patted his trusty companion on the head.

"Hey Ol' Bo," he said as he scratched the dog under his muzzle and around his floppy ears, "you're not gonna make fun of my outfit, are ya? Are ya?"

The dog brought happiness back to the man. Without him the old man would have died of loneliness, and he knew it. They both depended on the other.

Above the mantle of the fireplace, just under the mount of the eight-pointer, resting on two deer hooves, was a Marlin .30–30 Model 1893. The old man was a Marlin guy through and through. It was a no nonsense, no frills, come into my kitchen and I'll drop you where you stand kind of rifle. And when others traded up their weaponry for a new model that was factory shined with fancy stock, the old man said no thanks. Over the years, countless numbers of hunts were started and finished with this rifle, including the mount above the fireplace. The walnut stock was faded and scratched, which only added to its luster as a weapon that had been put into service time and time again. It had been retired over the mantle some years before and taken down only for an occasional cleaning and some target practice; here is where it rested only to be looked upon with fond memories for all the hunts that were conducted with it. The old man took the rifle off the wall and inspected it. He held it in his hands, feeling the grip of the stock, putting his index finger lightly on the trigger, and holding it at his side as if getting ready to bring it up to his shoulder to take a shot at a running buck. The rifle felt heavy in his hands, and the thought crossed his mind one last time whether he should go out or not. But when a man gets a taste of doing what he loves, it is hard to take the spirit from the man even if the man is old, and the thought of whether he should go disappeared for the time being.

He stood in the middle of the den fully dressed in hunting clothes he had not worn in many years, holding a 30–30 that had not been fired at big game in nearly the same amount of time, and he just stood there and thought. He tried to remember his last time in the woods deer hunting. It was the season just before her death. She was already diagnosed and very sick. He wasn't gone long. Just long enough to take his mind off things. It was a cold hunt. *It was all so cold,* he thought. Other than that he could not remember much about it. For the first time he pondered his age and what that otherwise insignificant number meant on a cold November day in the woods. November, the season where regardless of temperature, either high or low, cold seems to eventually penetrate and seep deep into your bones if you're on a mountain for a full day. If he saw his buck early, on the low ledges of the mountain, and if his aim was good and the deer dropped right away, maybe he could have the deer out of the woods by midday. On the other hand, if his aim was off and his eyes rusty or hand unsteady, the deer might run and run and the old man would be forced to track it wherever it went. He never thought of the chase. Come to think of it, he never thought of the cold. He never thought of the steep, jagged ledges up past the first ledge or of the long drag back down the mountain. He never really thought of his age, that is, until now. Holding the rifle in his hands, the old man realized for the first time just how much had been blocked out. So many things tucked away deep into his subconscious where he wouldn't have to think of them. And now he would have to. He would have to think it all through because he owed that much to the deer and the land and to his father and all that he had taught him. Himself, not so much, he thought. He gave up caring about the old man he occasionally saw in the mirror long, long ago. The others, however, they were different. They meant something, even if only in spirit. He held the rifle tight in his hands. *It's too early in the morning for doubt*, he thought, *and too late in the season for caution.*

"Let be done what will be done."

The old man looked at his reflection in the window.

"Let be done what will be done, for you and I may not meet again."

He whispered the words again and again. The words stuck even as his eyes pulled away from his own reflection to be replaced by the buck staring out on him from above the fireplace.

"But might you and I meet once more? I would like that. Indeed I would like that."

The big eyes on the wall above the mantle cast a frozen stare out on the old man. *Was it all that long ago?* the old man thought, as he stared back at the head with the neat, compact horns.

"That was one of my proudest days in the woods."

It was a long hunt that ended with the running buck gliding through the woods with outstretched strides. The shot caught the buck open in between some white birch saplings on the first ledge of Jenkins Mountain, downing him almost instantaneously. It really was that long ago, the old man concluded. It was long ago, and it was perfect. Perfect because everything was right there, right in front of him. The life he remembered was that of an exuberant young man with all the energy the world could offer, hunting the hills of his youth in search of the bounding young buck to present to his beautiful wife and family. It was perfect because of all the warm and caring faces that would share with him the day. It was a mug of hot coffee and a warm fireplace to sit next to when he returned from the woods after a cold day. And while the kids gathered round and their mother fixed him a plate of hot food, he would tell the story. The story was of the day. The story was of "The Hunt."

"Well, Ol' Bo, I've just about run out of folks to tell my stories to."

The Brittany looked on the old man with wide eyes and a cocked head and tried his best to understand.

"It's okay, Bo. It's okay. I'm gonna go anyway. I gotta good feeling about this season. Like a ballplayer entering his final spring training, I'm gonna give it my best 'cause I think I got a shot at the prize. I just got to finesse it, Ol' Bo. That's what I got to do, finesse it. I won't waste all my energy in one day. I'm gonna hunt smart."

He cradled the Marlin under his right arm and pulled his gloves from his hunting coat.

"It's getting late; where's my hat?"

On a hook in a hallway closet was his hat, a red wool cap with thin black checkered lines running through it. The crown of the hat was matted, and the bill of the cap was short and flat. The old man put on the cap, thus completing the outfit, and out the kitchen door he went. The dog followed but wasn't permitted out the door, as it closed quickly in front of him.

Chapter 7

AT QUARTER TO five the countryside was still asleep. The morning echoed silence as the old man walked across a small patch of yard to his truck. A sudden slight breeze crept in from the north and tickled the few leaves still left on some pin oaks, their desiccated, shriveled skins made hollow rattling sounds against the cover of darkness. Stars floated deep in the black, overcast sky and the moon sat low in the east and its light peeked in through the naked skeleton of a hickory tree, giving the early morning a haunting quality. The old man opened the driver's door to the pickup, leaned the rifle against the passenger seat, climbed in, and put the key in the ignition. Like a lion's growl in a church cathedral, the cold steel cut through the morning as the engine turned over and echoed through the valley. The engine was hoarse and grumbled as the pickup backed out of the driveway to take the old man to the land where deer roamed like giants. Once on the road, the old man pulled the knob on the dash and the dim lights turned on. The little pickup rattled on down the bumpy, pothole-filled road toward Jenkins' farm.

He had so looked forward to this day ever since Bo jumped the big buck back in October, and now the day was here. The old man figured that if he wanted to see the big buck, he would have to hunt deep into the upper ledges of the mountain where the cover was thickest and other hunters would be scarce. The big buck that had caused so much damage to the maple would most surely not be roaming around once daylight hit. Maybe by chance he might spot him just at sunup on the lower ledge enroute to his home deep in the heart of the mountain.

My best chance, the old man thought, *at seeing him down low might be at sunup on the lower ledge. After that he'll be long gone until dusk. He could also hole up in the swamp. That could be a possibility. Either way, the first ledge might be a nice spot to catch him. I'll plan on getting a glimpse of him as he's making his way back into deep cover or heading down into the swamp. After all, he didn't get that big by staying out in the open.*

It was unfortunate but true that the majority of hunters worked the low ledges, content to hunt the smaller bucks. The young bucks inexperience, sex drive, and curiosity brought them out in the open for easy pickoffs for a hunter up from the city just itching to kill anything with a horn. This was not the type of hunt the old man wanted, but his cautious side was beginning to get the best of him. He talked to himself.

"Well, it's the first day of the season, and I'll just take it easy and post on the lower ledges just up from the apple orchard and see how the deer are moving."

Just then, out of the corner of his eye, he could make out an object moving through the edge of a field just beyond the reaches of the truck's beaming lights. He eased on the brakes, slowing down to a crawl, when suddenly a blur of tan and white darted across the road.

"What is it? I don't know what that was, but it was big, that's for sure."

The old man's adrenaline meter began to rise, and his palms began to sweat in his gloves. He peered out the passenger side window into the field crossing where the tan object had disappeared and simultaneously put his foot on the gas and just as the truck began to accelerate, he turned his attention back to the road. Without warning, out of nowhere in the beams of light out fifteen yards in the middle of the road was an eight-point buck staring straight in through the windshield at the old man.

"Holy Moses," the old man hit the brakes and the truck skidded to a stop.

"Well, would ya look at that," he said as the buck jumped up and aired across the right half of the road, its white flag and hind legs disappearing over a line ditch of shrubs. The truck was motionless in the middle of the road, its driver in shock. The moment set the old man back by ten years. The truck raced down pancake hollow road. The excitement was in the old man's heart. He was anxious to get to Jenkins' farm to begin the hunt.

At 5:00 AM the old man pulled into the driveway of Jenkins' farm and parked the pickup in the usual spot under the maple tree. Before walking the driveway up to the wagon trail, he stopped at the farmhouse and checked the farmer's thermometer that was hanging from a post on the back porch just outside the kitchen door. An outdoor lantern hanging from an iron crossbar just under the pitch of the porch roof shined just enough light for the old man to make out the temperature at thirty five degrees.

"Not so bad," the old man thought, and to the wagon

trail he went. He walked the trail up between the north and south orchards in virtual darkness. The moon and the evening star—Venus was sitting just behind the eastern slope of Jenkins Mountain—still shone bright, and a line of clouds were rolling in from the north.

"We're gonna get a cold rain, it looks like."

A warm front was moving in, and the old man could see the clouds begin to settle low on the mountain. The peak of the great hill was beginning to disappear under the blanket of clouds and with it the moon and the Venus star. By five thirty he had made his way to the wood line of the hill and stopped to catch his breath, as was his custom. Staring down into the valley he noticed two lights, one from the back porch of the farm house and the other from the kitchen window. *It's nice to know,* the old man thought, *that another human is actually up this early.* It was Abraham Jenkins, of course, who was beginning his workday on the farm. "He's late," the old man gasped with an out-of-breath laugh. "I'll have to let him know next time I see him." As he stood on the hilltop, his senses also picked up on the smell of hickory smoke from the farmhouse chimney. The breeze was slight but steady coming out of the northwest. He decided to post the western slope. There was a nice trail there that a big buck might use. If he could get to the area before sunup, there might be an opportunity to see his buck come through the woods on his way to bed down. If he could position himself downwind, his chances would be good. The buck may not smell him out and take a different route home for bedding. The strategy of the woods was calling him home. The old man was excited to be on the hill, excited to be on his way into the woods, the woods of his youth.

Many of his hunting buddies had long since passed with the exception of Tony, and his health was failing him to where he could only hunt from a stand and still needed the supervision of one of his sons, usually his oldest boy Johnny.

Taking four cartridges from his gun belt, he opened up the lever action and cranked them in. As he loaded up it occurred to him that he had probably walked the trail from the orchards below more than a thousand times throughout his lifetime. He stood at the top of the hill and thought for a moment of when he was a boy hunting with his father and older brothers so many years ago.

His father was a carpenter who enjoyed walking the woods as much as working with a fine piece of ash or oak, some of which had been harvested from Jenkins Mountain. He taught his sons to appreciate the land through hunting. Spring, summer, and early fall were reserved for fly fishing the great streams of the Catskills, while the latter part of the autumn months were for bird and deer hunting. In those days, Elmer's father, along with his three brothers, rode a buckboard pulled by a plow horse the distance over to Jenkins farm, which was just one of many farms that attracted deer and gave protection for the sporting birds. Samuel Jenkins, the grandson of Abraham Jenkins the first, thought it a favor of the carpenter and his sons to harvest the property of the beasts that ate the apple saplings. Mrs. Jenkins concurrently agreed that they hunt the deer that ate the beans and peas she had painstakingly planted in back of the house during the spring. And so year after year they hunted the farm and the mountain with much success.

Elmer's father was an earnest man and demanded

discipline from his young boys if they were to hunt with him. The youngest did not carry a rifle his first time out, for there were not enough for everyone. Young Elmer started out with his father and brothers as they made their way along the trail and over the small wooden bridge. The boys watched the Pancake Hollow brook as it rushed under, sometimes fast if there had been a lot of rain, sometimes slow if the summer and fall were hot and dry, and sometimes not at all when the brook froze during the latter part of the deer season. Often the youngest would fall behind and his father would call to him.

"Elmer," he would say, "you'll never learn to hunt if you can't keep up. Come on, son. Come on, son, keep with your brothers."

They would walk up by the barn and the father would stop and watch as his sons fed the plow horses that came out to the corral fence line to visit the passersby. They would then continue up the hill between the stone walls that ran along the apple orchards, one to the north side of the trail and one to the south side, right up to the top of the hill. They would rest at the top and take in the valley of apple trees and farm country from which they had come. After some time had passed, the father and his sons would disappear into the woods, except for the youngest, who would remain behind, fascinated at how massive the rolling fields of Jenkins' farm was compared to his little world, the world of an eight-year-old boy. He would remain alone on that hill lost in this world, staring down into the valley at the little barn and farmhouse far, far away until his brothers would come back for him,

"Come on, Elmer! Come into the woods, Elmer!"

And now he was the only one left to walk the hill

and hunt the mountain. The last remaining brother, the only living son. And he stood on that hill. He stood alone staring down into the valley with the same fascination for the massive farm that he had more than half a century before. The land had not changed much, but he had. He had gotten older, he thought, but the land, the land was still the same. Before the moment could get the best of him, he turned and disappeared into the woods.

Chapter 8

THE TRAIL FROM the field passed into the woods until it became a part of what past generations called Jenkins Pass. But there were not many left who called it that anymore. Over the many years since the property was originally settled by Abraham Jenkins the first, other paths, wood roads, and logging trails had been made, leaving the route of Jenkins Pass the least desirable and most treacherous. It was still a trail used by the deer and other animals, at least one old hunter, and an occasional motorbike daredevil, one of Abraham's fifth generation grandsons, who taunted the edges of steep rock ledges with reckless abandon when he wasn't helping his father on the farm.

The old man walked the trail in the dark, heading north for about three hundred yards until the trail turned and started east, cutting up into the lower north end of the mountain. He took the trail up a steep, rocky hill that cut the first rock ledge in two. Once on top, he stopped in the middle of the trail to catch his breath. He pulled a handkerchief out of his coat pocket, took off his cap, and wiped his head of the beads of perspiration. The heavy hunting coat felt terribly uncomfortable as it did not breathe and so he took it off and tucked it under his arm. He wiped as much of the sweat from his head and neck as he could, not wanting it to run cold on his body, and then put the coat on again. Following the narrow, rocky trail in the dark, through the black of the woods, would be a difficult task for most hunters, even those who were younger and in better physical condition than the old man. But he was used to these woods, and this trail in particular he used countless times on former hunts. Even in the darkness of the woods where only the dimly lit moon glowing through the clouds and the trees could guide him, the old man found his way. With each step he felt the trail and recognized each marker along its route; a rock here, a dried up mud hole there, a root from a giant pin oak tree only half-buried across the trail. These were all signposts for the hunter, and they were just as good as the light of day. Landmarks such as these lined the entire length of the trail, and the old man recognized each one. He prided himself on maneuvering over the rough and winding stretch. After resting for a spell on top of the first ledge, the old man proceeded off the trail and in through the denser line of hardwoods. It was difficult to see, but he made his way south along the middle of the first ledge. His feet touched down lightly into the soggy leaves, as by now it had begun to rain. The old man was grateful to be in the woods, as the trees, even though their branches were empty, still offered more protection than the open fields below. By six thirty, he had made it to the edge of the hard wood at a spot where a hollowed out shag hickory had fallen some years earlier. This was the spot the old man was seeking, for it gave good cover for a post overlooking a thicket of spruce trees. Some thirty yards into the thicket was the blowdown where the Brittany had spooked the buck and two does earlier in the fall. To the east, along a buck trail, between the blowdown and the second ledge of the mountain, were a series of rubs and scrapes, including the one that raised the old mans eyebrows some weeks before. On the west side of the blowdown, the buck trail continued on a slight decline, grading downward toward the rough, rocky terrain of the first ledge where the trail turned abruptly and paralleled the ledge, running south. On this part of the trail were many rubs as well, and the hunter remembered them from previous bird seasons. The trail would eventually turn west again and dip down through a narrow crevasse in the first ledge and out into the south field of Jenkins' apple farm.

The morning was becoming cold and wet, though the clouds gave a brief respite from the rain. The old man was wet with perspiration from his long walk, and so he rested his rifle against the rotted out hollow of the massive tree and took off his hat and coat. With his handkerchief he once again wiped his head and neck of sweat and then put on his clothes and readjusted his belt. The break of dawn was not yet ready to set in on the mountain. The sounds of water droplets fell from the tree branches to the bed of leaves covering the floor of the woods. Sitting on a broken limb of the hickory and nestled in between a bigger limb and the trunk of the tree provided the perfect lookout for the hunter to rest and await the break of day and the prize he sought.

The water droplets grew plump on the tree branches high above the ground. Each droplet clung to a branch until it got too fat and could not cling anymore. Then slowly it would sag from its branch until gravity got the best of it, and the swollen droplet would go for a free fall to the earth, where it pattered on the floor of the woods. In the still of the early morning, each drop echoed. Throughout, there were hundreds, maybe thousands of droplets swelling, sagging, and falling all at different times, making the same pattering sound. The old man listened to the sounds, occasionally catching a heavy water droplet on the bill of his hunting cap or on his ears that stuck out from beyond his cap, and he would wipe it off, all the while trying to be still as the trees and quiet like the rocks under the leaves.

He pulled from his coat a pocket watch and raised it up close to his eyes and squinted to try and read it, but it was still too dark and he couldn't make out where the big hand was. *Must be close to seven*, he thought, but overcast skies made it seem a lot earlier. Patiently he sat and listened to the droplets pattering down on the leaves. Eyes, once keen, stared straight ahead through the darkness in the direction of the clusters of spruce. After many minutes went by, the old man noticed a change in the woods. For the first time he could make out the silhouettes of trees off in the distance not far away. He judged they were maybe ten feet in front of him, and with each minute that went by, he could see a little farther and then farther still. First it was a few saplings only many feet away, and then a bigger tree still a bit farther. And then a group of trees and a rock outcropping some distance farther, and then finally in view of the hunter came the moment he dreamed of for so many years.

In his youth, when the seasons changed from the hot of summer to the cool crisp evenings of the fall, Elmer would lay in his bed at night and think of the deer season still to come. It was always the beginning of the hunt that his restless mind clung to, walking the hills in the dark of the wee morning hours, climbing up through the ledges with a rifle slung over his shoulder, nestling in to post at the base of a downed tree or along a rock wall. And as he fell asleep in his bed, he dreamed of the woods growing light as he peered into the bedroom where a magnificent buck stood proud.

The old man's breath grew heavy as he held his rifle tight in his hands, cocked at an angle with the butt between his forearm and resting on his leg and the barrel, nose up at forty-five degrees. The clusters of spruce ahead of him had not quite come into view to where each tree and branch had detail, but instead the mass ahead of him could only be identified as no more than a black hole in the middle of the hunter's field of view. It was as if a painter had crafted his canvas complete with dull dreary charcoals that made a silhouette of the woods and then ripped out the center of his work so that there was nothing, just a hole in the center of the canvas. No shadows and no light. But the shelters of trees were there and the old man waited intensely for them to come into view. The hill of the first ledge was getting warmer, and a fog began to rise up from the valley below. It crept along, contouring the lay of the land, slowly rising up through the trees as it went. Luckily for the hunter, it was only a light fog and he thought it not a significant threat to his vision, as he could still make out the black hole in front of him and the other trees and landmarks to either side. After a period of time, the fog grew patchy and dense in some areas, like clouds rising up the landscape, and the hunter suddenly grew wary that all would be well.

The woods reluctantly welcomed daybreak, and for the first time he could see in through the spruce, but only briefly in between the clouds of fog that continued on by and up the rest of the mountain. The clusters of spruce were thick and full and even on their lower branches the needles were healthy and rich in density and ranged for some distance along the first and second ledges of the mountain. The old man's post on the fallen hickory was at the foot of the northernmost part of these spruce clusters and from this post the hunter was some twenty-five yards from the blowdown. It was this section of the spruce clusters where many of the trees had been snapped in two from a blizzard some years earlier. These fallen spruce were bigger than the others, and so their big sweeping branches had accumulated the many inches of wet snow until their limbs couldn't support the weight anymore and snapped in two. Many storms contributed to the violence against the bigger spruce that lined the floor of the mountain, and the deer and other animals that lived here were the beneficiaries, as there could not have been a better place to hide and rest.

The hunter peered in from his post but only got small glimpses of a portion of the blowdown where two spruce had fallen and lay across one another. There were many branches from the two trees and others that precluded fair visibility into the thicket of the blowdown. The fog continued and this became a very poor filter for allowing light to pass through the first ledge of the mountain. The pattering of rain drops falling from the trees continued, but other than that, all was quiet. The animals of the woods were either tucked away in their beds or at least taking seclusion from the wet morning, and the old man, thinking it may take some time for conditions to improve, cradled his rifle in his arms and waited.

Upon checking the time, the hunter turned his attention once again to the line of spruce and the trail to the east and west of the blowdown. At twenty-five after seven, there was a problem. The woods were quiet and still; the fog continued to rise up from the valley; the pattering of raindrops continued to pound on the floor of the woods, and nature had made its second call to the old man. He had had to go for the last hour or so and knew that he should have went before day broke, but he was too excited to get into the woods and to his spot overlooking the blowdown that he forgot. Thankfully, the woods were soaked from the early morning rain, so he could move with little noise. From his seat on the hickory, he turned and looked behind him for a suitable place to go. Another young hickory a few yards behind him seemed as good a place as any. He rested his rifle at his post and proceeded. His intention wasn't to conceal himself, for there was no reason for that, as he was alone in the woods, but rather to conceal the odor of human urine if it was at all possible to do so. Some hunters believed that human urine actually attracted animals, including deer in rut, but this old deer hunter had no thoughts either way on the subject. He stepped carefully, not wanting to arouse the woods with the crackling of a twig or the shuffling of wool pants until he reached the young hickory.

Going to the bathroom during deer season was an arduous task, due to the many layers of clothing. First the belt, then the wool pants, followed by the unsnapping of the long johns. Aside from this, for the male species there is only one other act of true and natural gratification involving the organ that stands with the act of urinating outdoors. For the old man, it was one of those fringe benefits of being a man, and he reveled in it. A chill ran up the hunter's spine as he drained onto the base of the hickory, the rifle cradled across one arm. The hair on the back of his neck stood on end as he looked up through the branches of the many trees and into the heavens. The fog was thick and he could barely make out the roof of the woods, for it was concealed in the cloud cover.

"What a beautiful morning," he whispered as he continued to hose down the tree, "the weather is just right for deer to be on the move right about now. If it stays clear enough for me to get a shot off, just clear enough for one shot, that's all I need, just one at the big one. He'll come through, I think."

Steam rose from the base of the hickory and the smell of urine was in the air. After snapping up, zipping up, putting on and readjusting his belt, the old man turned to walk back to his post. He barely took more than a single step, however, for there in the trail just west of the cluster of spruce, carefully making its way up the hill toward the blowdown, was a deer, its upper body hidden behind the blanket of fog. He could make out little more than its tan legs, just below the line of fog, moving against the calm of the woods, each hoof planting into the wet leaves as it graded its way up the hill. The hunter's heart pounded against his body the instant his eyes perceived movement of the figure drifting up with the fog, and he stood there frozen, a lump in his throat. The deer kept walking up the hill toward the line of spruce, checking the air every few steps along the way. The hunter had to take a breath; he had to let it all out. All that was bottled up inside, all the excitement was at the ready to come bursting out of him. The intensity to find out what it was in the woods that was walking toward him was too much to endure. Was it a buck? Was it the big one, maybe the one that Bo jumped when bird hunting? Or maybe it's the one that scuffed up the maple tree. Midway between the line of spruce and the point at which the old man had first encountered the tan legs, the deer stopped. The tan legs stood as motionless as the base of the tree saplings, and the fog continued on up the hill. The old man thought the deer may have figured him out. The deer must have seen him, smelled him, and sensed him. Some twenty yards apart, the two stood frozen, separated only by fog and some tree saplings.

The deer's lower quarters were still visible, but that was all that he could make out. He planted his foot and carefully shifted his weight onto his lead foot and felt the soft cushion on the floor of the woods. *Thank God for the rain,* he thought. He took two more long steps and carefully reached for his rifle.

"Just stay calm, my deer, stay calm."

The fog was clearing even more quickly, and as the hunter divided his sights between his rifle and the deer, he caught a rather quick glimpse of an eye, like that of a bull, black and cold, peering at him from a break in the mist. The eye staring at him through the mist left an indelible mark on his nerves. The stare was intense, almost beady, and so cold that the old man thought it must be the big buck he was looking for. The fog got lighter, but was still just heavy enough that the old man had to orient himself and squint hard to bead in on his target. As he did so, he touched his finger to the trigger and made ready his body for the recoil of the Marlin. Another break in the fog was approaching, and he knew this to be his best opportunity of the entire morning, and so as the last patch of fog glided up the hill he inhaled a deep breath and held it as the woods in front finally opened up. His eyes grew large and his finger pressed into the trigger, but there was no trophy buck in his sights. He shifted the trunk of his body slowly to the left in the direction that the fog was moving, over toward the blowdown, but still nothing.

"That's funny," he thought, *"I didn't hear him run."*

Carefully, he lowered the rifle to his chest and listened. The woods fell hypnotically quiet, and the old man briefly thought his hearing had been lost. He saddled the fallen hickory and then swung his right leg over the massive trunk that embodied his post and walked out beyond it toward an opening halfway between the hickory and the blowdown. He raised the rifle three quarter high, turned to his right, and hawkishly peered on down the hill, but again saw nothing. The slight breeze continued its pursuit up the hill and the old man closed his eyes as it swept across his face and he breathed it in through his nose. He let it all out and sniffed at the air, this time paying close attention to the various smells that entered his nostrils. Deer that are on the move give off a scent, and so the old man sniffed several times, hoping to sniff up the brute smell of the buck that could have possibly backtracked down the hill. Unfortunately for him, he could smell only the unmistakable lure of the plentiful spruce and hemlock.

Well, he thought, *no trace of the deer going up the hill, and no trace of him going down the hill, so that means he either went south away from me, or he's right here.*

The hunter turned and looked straight into the blowdown. The objective of hunting the ledge in the early morning hours was of course to head off a buck before he got to the bedding area. The blowdown itself would be difficult to hunt, for it was thick and wild and left too many escape routes for the deer, leaving a hunter hung out to dry. He walked into the blowdown but got no farther than that day in the fall when he and Bo put up the grouse and jumped the buck and two does. There he stopped and contemplated. This place was vast and mysterious, dark and rugged, with massive trees, mostly spruce and hemlock, which were uprooted or snapped in two from the many storms and high winds that whipped up the great hill. Some trees stood tall, but their many limbs were either broken or laying strewn across the forest floor, or sagging to create dark caves for the inhabitants to seek shelter in. Complimenting the fortress were the streamlined thickets of briars and long, thorny wild rose and bramble bushes that acted, to near perfection, as barbed wire would, keeping out any unwanted guests.

"I'm not going to walk into his house uninvited," the old man thought with a whisper, "for if I break in the front, I'll only get a glimpse of his tail fly'n out the back. No, I think I'll walk the outer edge and work my way all around the blowdown and back to my post at the old hickory."

He walked close to the line of hemlock and spruce and thorny bushes that made the outer perimeter of the blowdown. Frequently, the hunter stopped and posted, hoping to get a glimpse of a bedded down buck and careful not to startle its inhabitants. It was less difficult to walk quietly, as the rain had soaked the floor of the woods, so he was content to post and walk. The blowdown extended south quite a ways, and the old man followed it in that direction. Every so often he stopped and posted for a while before moving on. About a half hour after he started afoot, he heard a gunshot. It came from the south, and the old man judged the distance of the booming sound to be down near the beaver pond. And then there came another shot, followed by yet another.

His initial reaction was one of anger. It angered him to know that he was sharing the woods with another hunter. But at the same time, he felt ashamed that he may have missed his opportunity, or at least what could have been, as he was not sure the deer he saw in the fog was his buck. *But it could've been,* he thought, and as far as he was concerned, that meant it was. Even worse, the buck that was his could've gotten spooked and ran south toward the beaver pond right into the waiting sights of the other hunter. The old man shook his head in utter disappointment.

"I may have helped that asshole out!"

He kicked at the wet leaves and unbuttoned his wool coat.

"That might just be my deer down there, and it wouldn't surprise me one bit if it was," he whispered as he wiped a bead of sweat from his forehead, his frustration beginning to get the best of him.

Up ahead, just past the blowdown, was a stonewall that ran east to west through the first ledge of the mountain and down to the apple farm. It was a part of many walls that could be found on Jenkins Mountain and were made by Abraham Jenkins the first when constructing the Jenkins Pass trail. The old man decided to sit on the wall and post for a spell, hoping that if the deer escaped the gunshots that it might head back in his direction. It wasn't out of the realm of possibilities for a buck to run between two hunters, and so he rested and waited for the woods to come alive.

Only moments after taking his seat on the wall overlooking a line of birch and elm, the old man heard the sounds of branches and twigs snapping in the foreground. He dropped to one knee and raised the gun chest high and prepared for the approaching sounds. In the distance, he thought he saw the dancing of tan and white dodging through the trees. First one doe came running, and then another, and another, followed by yet another. It was a total of four does as far as he could tell. They were no longer running at a full gait, for they had run some distance and were beginning to slow down in the thick of trees. They were now down to a trot and moving directly toward the old man. Closing in, about forty yards away, which was no small distance in the woods, the four does turned east and started their slow accent up the hill toward the second ledge. The rocky outcroppings between the first and second ledge were full of cedar, hemlock and spruce. The old man, after satisfying himself that no bucks were in the area, guessed that the does would probably stay the course until they reached the thick of green between the two ledges.

"Well," the old man whispered, "if there's a buck on their trail, he should be coming through shortly, that is, if that asshole down there didn't bag him already."

He took a seat on the wall and waited as patiently as a hunter could, considering the current situation, though the emotional highs and lows were almost too much for him to bear. Transfixed by his surroundings, his eyes pleaded with the trees for a buck to come into view.

"This is what hunting is all about," he continued to tell himself with clinched teeth, "just got to be patient."

He reached into his pocket and pulled from it his watch. The time read quarter to ten. Looking south toward where the does had come through, there was movement once more. One lone deer was approaching with its head low to the ground. The old man took a knee once again and remained as still as he could, using the stone wall as his backdrop. The deer kept coming, moving slow but steady, sneaking this way and that way through the trees. The old man thought he saw horns, but then again, it could have been the branches of trees playing their same old tricks on his eyes. When the deer came within forty yards, he stopped and lifted his head, most likely not to show off his compact rack of eights, but to sniff the air out of concern. The hunter was ready and shouldered his rifle. The buck showed no signs of alarm and turned his proud little head toward the east in the direction of the does that had passed through. The old man locked his eye in on the sights that bore down on the buck's back shoulder. With his finger poised on the trigger, the hunter was ready to take his prize. Hands were steady, eyes were keen, breathing controlled, and the buck had framed himself to near perfection. The hunt was all but complete. One shot and it would all be done. But it would not be done. The hunter lowered his rifle slowly to his chest. "You're a proud little buck," whispered the old man, "but you're not the one I'm looking for. Maybe next year." The buck headed east up the hill slow but steady and then out of sight. "He'll be a big buck if hunters like me give him some time to grow. Maybe he'll be the future of this mountain."

The woods grew quiet once again. *What a morning,* thought the old man. Several deer had come through, one of which was an impressive little buck. The old man was rejuvenated. The excitement had almost been too much for him. His heart pounded and beads of sweat ran from his forehead. He removed his cap and took from his coat a handkerchief and wiped his bald head. Back and forth over the top of his head he rubbed the white cloth, again and again. With eyes closed, almost in a meditative state, he ran the cloth over his face, and then with the same hand massaged his temples in a slow circular motion. Over and over he did this, and it relaxed him, and slowly he began to slow down from the morning that was.

"All right," he whispered to himself, "We're onto something. I haven't seen the big one, but the deer are moving right around me. I'm moving along a-okay, and if I choose, I'll make it to that second ledge if I need to give chase to a running buck."

"Ahh," he said with a half laugh, "I might as well not think much about that right now, 'cause if he comes through, I'll take 'em from where I sit, and until that time comes I'm going to relax and enjoy being in the woods, a deer hunter once again."

With that, he ran the handkerchief over his head once more and pulled his cap down over his head until the brim sat just above his eyebrows and the rim of the cap snugged under the tops of his ears.

Just then, another shot rang out from the same direction as the last. Once again the old man's heart became a pit in his throat and his veins pulsated through the many layers of cotton and wool. He peered south through the woods in the direction of the shot, holding the rifle tight across his waist. "Who the fuck is doin' all that shootin' down there?"

In the scheme of things, it was really inconsequential who was in the woods doing the shooting. It was not out of the ordinary to see or hear another hunter in the woods, or on a mountain, especially if the hill to be hunted had road access. The old man, an experienced hunter and lifelong pupil of these woods, knew this to be the case, and so his resentment for another man simply because he was lucky enough to have a shot at a deer and the old man hadn't used his opportunity wasn't justifiable behavior. Deep inside he knew this to be true. The hunting game was not a fair game. Not every hunter, no matter how prepared or experienced, would get a clear look at a buck. Unlike the game of football where each team gets four downs and the opportunity to score is eminent, or a baseball game where a team gets three outs every inning and the chance to score is always just one swing of the bat away, the hunting game may seem a bit bleak by comparison. From the deers standpoint, if they had an opinion to voice, the hunter's chances were not only fair, but obviously stacked against the home team.

In the distance, two squirrels chased each other up and down a shag hickory tree and then around it several times before darting off through the woods. This was the only movement made by any creature, including the old man who sat on the wall solid and still as any rock that existed on the great hill. After some time had passed, he satisfied himself that no buck had gotten past the hunter from the south. He remained on the wall for another hour and passed the time away by eating an early lunch, which consisted of a peanut butter sandwich, a corn muffin, one square cut of burnt scrapple leftover from breakfast, a bruised apple compliments of Jenkins' orchard, and a tangerine, which he found always complemented a meal, as the sandwich and muffin had parched his throat. Eating in the woods offered him the occasion for further reflection. The entire mountain afforded to the old man its share of special memories, but from where he now sat, he thought upon one from when he was a boy. He remembered one of the early lessons his father taught him and his brothers about hunting. Only the woods, the old man surmised, could bring back memories from so long ago and give them as much clarity as if they happened only yesterday. The old man gazed about at the trees. His mind drifted off.

Chapter 9

WHEN HE WAS a boy, his father taught him and his older brothers to follow up the first shot taken at a deer, or as his father would clarify, the first shot at a buck, for he reminded his boys again and again that he disapproved of shooting does. The idea was to discipline the hunter to track the animal carefully and skillfully. Being a carpenter took great skill and patience, and so his craft was never performed hastily. The same virtues were extolled on hunting and fishing. A patient hunter did not, under any circumstances, chase a buck after taking a shot, but would instead go to the area where the buck stood at the time of the shot and examine the ground for blood, bone, hair, and any other clues that might be left behind. It was a tried and true way of picking up a blood trail at the very beginning and tracking it right to the end. His father would brag, "Boys, I've never lost a buck in the woods because I always followed up my first shot."

It was on an October drive on Jenkins Mountain back in 1894 that young Elmer's mind gravely betrayed him, and the old man, right up to the present day, grew weak when he thought about it. It was about a half hour from dusk when the buck stepped out from behind an elm in the hardwoods on the south side of the second ledge. His brothers had put on a drive that started from the beaver pond, out into a flat of hardwood, and then up the hill. Many deer were kicked out of hiding, including two bucks, the smaller of which had made its way right up into a dense crop of young elm and other hardwoods, each only a few feet apart. The boy's post was directly on the other side of these saplings. A figure, maybe more than one, as the boy could not see for sure, was moving through the trees, about fifty yards ahead of him. The deer moved in slowly and cautiously, continually turning and looking behind in the direction from which he had come. As he approached to within thirty yards, the boy squinted and with much effort, due to trickery from the branches, counted it to be a small but impressive five-point buck. The buck stopped for some time at a big old elm, and the boy took aim and waited for the buck's next move. When the buck stepped out from behind the elm, the boy was ready and wasted little time. He beaded in his front sight so that it rested deep in the "V," planted the barrel right on the belly of the buck, and squeezed the trigger. The rifle echoed a bellowing boom and had a ferocious kick that damn near separated the boy's shoulder and almost knocked him off his feet. The sound shook the trees and clouded the hill in smoke. As the boy reclaimed control over his balance and peered carefully in through the smoke and trees, the deer jumped and ran hard heading east. The boy instinctively ran after it. The confused deer ran parallel to him and continued east. Running in plain sight of the deer, he legged it out with him all the way, tail flagging as it went, only about thirty-five yards away. He needed an opening in the woods to take his next shot and soon he would get one, for up ahead, perpendicular to their advances, was the Jenkins Pass trail. The boy's orientation was phenomenal, and sensing the trail ahead, stopped on a buffalo nickel, planted his feet, raised the gun to his shoulder, and took aim. Just as the deer broke into the opening of the trail, the gun blared one final time. The earth shook, and the deer took one last great leap, and then belly flopped down onto the trail, dead as Mom's meatloaf, as his father liked to say. When the boy made it over to the trail to inspect his prize, he nearly jumped out of his boots. The supposed five-point buck laying in the trail, its four legs spread out in all directions, its tongue dangling out of its mouth with foam pasted across its chin and eyes glistening green to black, was not a buck at all, but instead a doe. The boy had shot a doe. There were no horns between her ears, only the bloody hole ripped open at her belly from the lead ball, and the boy crouched down beside her and put his head in his hands, full of shame for the grave mistake he had made.

After a short time had passed, he could hear the rustling of leaves from the woods behind him. It was two of his brothers walking up the hill. They had followed the sounds of gunfire. Upon viewing the site on Jenkins Pass, they could not help but feel sympathetic for their younger brother's misfortune and the quandary he now faced, as they were all very aware of their father's fiery tongue and stern criticisms of his sons.

That evening, back at their own farm, while hanging the doe from a thick cross beam in the barn with the help of his brothers, his father asked that he be left alone with his youngest son.

"Elmer," he said in a deep cutting voice, "why did you shoot this deer? Your brothers put on drive for you in the hopes that you would get a shot at a nice buck."

"I know, Pa," the boy said with an apologetic tone, "but I could've sworn I saw horns through the trees. I could see them close enough to count, and that's when I shot."

"And what happened?" asked the father.

"Well, when I took the first shot it sort of threw me a bit, and when I got on him again the deer was off and running, so I shot again."

"Were you on the deer with your first shot?" asked the father.

"Oh yes, Pa, I was on him all the way," replied the boy.

The father walked over and looked at the hanging doe and asked, "Then why is there only one hole in this deer?"

The boy stood alongside his father and just stared at the belly of the deer; he had no reply. His father sighed, patted his son on the back, and said, "Go in and get cleaned up for supper. Tomorrow were gonna go back on the hill where you were today."

The boy turned and with a bewildered stare asked, "But why, Pa?"

His father, with his back to the boy, grinned and kicked at some dirt on the barn floor as he walked out the door.

"'Cause I have something to show ya," he said as he continued on toward the house.

The next morning, before dawn broke, father and son were up and readying themselves for the day. The boy was still confused as to what good could possibly come from climbing half a mountain to retrace the steps of a hunt that had ended; the deer was already hanging in the barn. But if anything was true about the wee morning hours besides the dark and the cold, it was that the boy had enough common sense to know never to ask the same question twice of his father. And so it was to be that enlightenment would come soon enough, and hitching the wagon and riding with his father with the chill of the November morning winds burning his face would be a small price to pay for knowledge. These of course were not the boy's sentiments, but those of his father, and through years of discipline were now his by default. Upon reaching Jenkins' farm, the father asked his son, who was in command of the reigns, to continue on past the farmhouse and drive the wagon all the way to the top of the farm. The boy thought this a strange request, as horse and wagon were always parked just to the side of the farmhouse where the horse was better protected from the wind than on the open hill. The only time the wagon was ever parked on the top of the hill was when a deer was being loaded onto the buckboard, and the boy was sure that this wasn't the case on this morning, for his father had left his rifle at home. They made it to the top of the hill by sunup, and without stopping to view the lovely rolling landscape of Jenkins' apple farm in the early morning rays of first light, the two disappeared into the woods.

They headed south until they came upon the meadow flat just north of the beaver pond. From there they turned and headed northeast up the mountain, as it was easier than trying to traverse the jagged rocks of each ledge. By mid-morning, they reached the section of hard wood on the southern tip of the second ledge where the boy had posted the day before.

"Well, this is it," said the boy, pointing to the surrounding area.

"Over there about sixty yards is where I first saw the deer."

He pointed to the dense line of young trees.

"I had come up from the north side and posted on the other side of these elm, and the deer came right through here and stood behind that bigger elm, the one next to that slump of discolored leaves."

"Ya see it, Pa?" he pointed again, "Right down there about forty or so yards off."

"I see it, son," said his father, "but show me where you dropped the doe."

"Well," said the boy, "the pass trail runs around just over through those trees, and if we walk the trail we'll find right where I dropped her. There was a lot of blood and hair left on the trail."

"I'll bet there was," said his father, "let's go check it out."

They got to the trail and walked in silence, side by side, the boy carrying his rifle while his father kept his hands warm in his coat pockets. The boy finally broke the silence and said, "Pa, I'm really sorry for shootin' that doe, but I could've sworn I saw horns, and well, I guess I just wasn't payin' attention. But I just don't understand why we're up here doin' this. I mean, huntin's one thing, but you aren't even carryin' a rifle. I just don't get it."

"You will," said his father. "In a few minutes you'll understand."

They walked the trail about one hundred feet until they came to the spot where the deer had dropped. It was easy to find, as the ground was marked with leaves and rocks stained with blood and clumps of white hair and even some small, sinewy pieces of bone and cartilage, most likely from the ball breaking through the rib cage.

"Well, here it is, this is the spot," the boy said as he kicked at the bloodstained leaves. "I shot from over there," pointing to a hickory tree some thirty yards away.

His father nodded his head and seemed quite pleased with how effective the shot was. He thought for a moment, trying to visualize the events in his own mind, and then said in an inquisitive tone, "Now let's go over to where you took the kill shot."

The boy's nerves were getting to him; a feeling of guilt came over him as he broke out into a cold sweat. His father had a way of gathering information to build a case against his sons that was very useful, if not downright cruel. It was a prodding, plotting method that built up slow but clear; so very clear in its intent to find the story, to paint the whole picture and bring clarity, usually followed by swift justice. They walked to the hickory. The boy removed his cap, wiped the sweat from his forehead, and waited for his father's next move.

"Now, this is where you were," said his father, "and over there is where you first saw the buck."

He pointed in the direction of the bigger elm tree, the one that had the discolored leaves lying at its base. It was far off in the distance.

"And over there is where the deer was dropped with your second shot."

The father looked back and forth at the two points,

the first being the elm so far away, and the second being the trail that was only about thirty yards away.

"Son," he asked after a moment had passed, "where were you when you took the first shot? It could not have been from here, could it?"

"Well no, Pa. It was up ahead a ways," the boy pointed west toward an area closer to the elm tree.

"C'mon," said his father, "let's go have a look."

Together they walked closer to the spot of the elm with the discolored leaves at its base until the boy, looking around, recognized where he had posted.

"Right in here," he said, "this is the area where I was posting when the deer stepped out from that elm. I think I was standing right next to that leaning hickory."

He pointed to a shag hickory tree that had fallen through the "V" of another elm tree, creating some nice posting cover for a hunter.

"I took my first shot from here, and when the deer ran …."

There was silence as the boy fought for the words, not wanting to say it, not wanting to admit his wrong-doing.

"Anyway, after the first shot the deer ran, and I went after it until it broke into the clearing of the trail, and then I shot again."

A feeling of relief came over the boy. It was out, the whole story was out, and whatever the matter may cost him, whatever punishment may be in store for him, it was out at last.

The boy's father stood next to him with one hand in his coat pocket and the other on the leaning hickory. He gazed toward the group of young elm trees off in the distance and the bigger elm with the discolored leaves at its base, and noticed that from where they stood the leaves were more tan than red and brown.

"Son," he asked, "how many times have I told you to follow up your first shot?"

The boy stared at the ground and did not answer. After a time, the father pulled from his coat pocket a rope and held it out under the boy's nose.

"Here, take this."

"What's this?" the boy asked with a bewildered look.

"Just take it and hand me over that rifle and walk with me over to that big elm."

The boy took the rope and handed his father the rifle.

A leaf on an elm rustled a hollow tone as a slight breeze whipped up from the west. It was a relief to the boy, and in an effort to cool down, he opened up his coat as he walked. A family of squirrels carried on up in a hickory not far away. They chased each other up and down the tree, cussing and screeching as they played. No regard or caution was given to the hunters that trespassed through their woods; they went about their business, happily enjoying the mid-morning sun. The boy's father walked on ahead of him until he was in plain sight of the bigger elm. When he came in clear view of it, he stopped suddenly and fixed his eyes near the base of the tree and waited for the boy to approach. The boy played with the rope as he walked and had almost completed a half-hitch knot by the time he got to where his father stood.

"It's up a little further, Pa," he said, looking up at his father.

His father did not say a word. Instead he stood nearly frozen, his eyes pasted at the sight at the base of the tree.

"What's wrong, Pa?"

The boy was confused as he looked up at his father. He followed the path of his eyes over to the base of the elm tree. As instantaneously as his eyes caught the tree, the hair on the back of his head stood straight up and a chill coursed down his back.

"Oh no," he proclaimed, and slid his hand up to his head and slowly grabbed at his cap.

"I don't believe it," he said, as he crouched down and looked on intently almost in tears from what he saw at the base of the elm.

There, at the base of the tree, nestled in the leaves was the tan and white mound that made up a deer. The boy got up and walked slowly over to the fallen deer, and as he drew closer he could make out the yellowish-white antlers that made up the sporting buck. The boy quickly pieced together what had happened. As he thought, he crouched down next to the deer and lifted the head up by its antlers to inspect the rack. It was a five-pointer; three tines on the right and two on the left. A third was starting about two inches off the base of the left antler, but was less than a half-inch in size. The antlers stood high and straight and the boy's father thought that it was probably a two-year-old and a future trophy in the making. All in all, a nice buck, he thought.

"Well, son, I've told you and your brothers before about following up your first shot, and now you know why. I'll see you back at the wagon. I'm gonna hunt my way back over the north end and then back on down to the field. I reckon it'll take you a good three hours to drag him on out."

With that he cranked open and closed the lever action and turned to walk away. The boy still crouched next to the buck, watched as his father turned his back. After a moment had passed, the boy asked enthusiastically,

"Pa, how did you know?"

His father turned back and with a proud look said, "Son, I've seen you shoot. You're a much better shot than your brothers; just inexperienced, that's all. I knew something must have went wrong for you to miss at a standing buck. The doe only had one hole in her and you claimed you dropped her with the second shot. I'll see ya back at the wagon."

The father turned again and started north, but only got a few steps before he stopped and turned to the boy.

"Hey son," he said, with a pride that only a father can have for his favorite son, "that's a nice buck. You drag it on out with pride, ya hear?"

Chapter 10

THE RIFLE RESTED cradled in his arms. The old man finished his lunch and pondered the exact group of trees that might have watched over his young five-point buck all those many years ago. *Like old friends*, he thought, *always here when we want to visit them.*

After the meal, which satisfied him thoroughly, he folded up neatly a wrinkled old brown paper bag that had held his lunches since the September bird season and put it back into his coat pocket. The tangerine peels he left on the stonewall and the apple core he flung side armed a few feet away. *Something for the chipmunks*, he thought, as he looked down at the tangerine peels.

The old man decided it was time to circle back through the blowdown and make his way to his original post at the fallen shag hickory. And so he set out to hunt the whole way back, paying close attention to the dense cover of thorns and bramble of the blowdown. Steps were taken with great care, and every so often he stopped, usually by a downed tree or cluster of birch, and soaked in the views, sounds, and scents of the woods around him. To his left was the heart of the blowdown. To the right was the gentle incline filled with elm and birch and shadowed by the sharp, protruding rocks that made up the shelf of the second ledge and the cedars and spruce that lined that ledge. Neither the blowdown nor the ledge was ignored by the old man, for he was sure that a buck could be on the move, checking for doe scent.

The clouds had moved off the mountain and rays of sunlight pushed through the boundaries of the woods. Every so often the old man stopped and posted. Much of the blowdown was impenetrable for a deer hunter to walk through. *It's a fortress, truly custom-built just for the wild animals,* he thought, for only the rabbit, the deer and the bobcat could move through it so efficiently without disturbing a single branch, leaf, or thorn. *With all that I know, I'm still powerless to enter into it.*

"All that I can do," he whispered, "is stand here on their back porch and wait for them to come out; if they come out at all!"

Looking toward the hill, he set his eyes on the rise of cedars and spruce creeping up the outcropping of the second ledge. A young doe moved among the trees. She ate some of the tender hemlock branches that were low enough for her to get to with only an extended neck. The hunter followed the happy white tail through the trees, but he was not the only one. On the edge of the blowdown, concealed behind the dense cover of green and thorny mast, was a big, burley buck. He distanced himself from the hunter. He edged his great rack right out to the edge of cover, but was reluctant to move any farther. Only fifty feet apart, separated by the confines of the blowdown, but the old man did not see. The slightest of sounds rattled from the buck's antlers as the great tines caught the brush and pulled it this way and that. But the old man heard only what his eyes were telling him he was hearing, and that was the doe with the happy tail. The hunter remained focused on the hemlock-filled ledge. The buck stood frozen with exhaustion. Its mind, normally smart, cautious, and strong-willed, was at present drowning in testosterone.

Chapter 11

THE BUCK WAS a rogue creature that had wandered off its stomping grounds, a square two-mile territory deep in the heart of the third ledge of Jenkins Mountain. There were no other bucks that were massive enough to challenge his kingdom, and he ruled it quite effectively with brute force and psychological torture. He was now entering his fourth rutting season and the third as the most dominant buck on the mountain and ruler of deer and all small creatures. His strength was proven in battle not just with those of his own kind, and there were many, but also in self-defense against the wolf, the coyote, and the bobcat, all of which suffered for their meager attempts at sustenance. Their needs were cruel and inconsequential compared to the severity of the only task in life for the male deer, to procreate. And this he did, and did well. For a buck in the wild, he had an obsession with greatness. Every beat of the heart under the blanket of hollow white chest hair was a beat for masculinity and the intense desire to pass on the seed of life to a keeper who could nurture and protect it, keep it warm and make it grow. And there were but only a few that could complete the mission of giving birth to his offspring. The seeds from him grew big inside the bellies of the does of Jenkins

Mountain, and some died while giving birth or shortly thereafter. For this reason, as if knowing the fateful outcome of his mates, he took to the hills high and low on a crusade to impregnate as many doe as possible through the peek of the rut, and in doing so find and mate the toughest females on the mountain. Rough and ready and hung bigger than and more genetically superior to any other buck on the mountain, this buck moved with a frenzy of the possessed. Shrouded in sweat and feces, its face pasted in a foamy saliva from its mouth to its ears and dribbling urine and semen down its hindquarters, this buck became to the hills, the standard bearer of the rugged and untamed, with the bloodline of royalty swelling between its legs and the crown of a king atop its head in the form of fourteen glorious points.

The rack sat high on the king's head and opened up and out, giving near perfect symmetry to either side. The beast's neck, a massive, swollen stump of fur and fat, broad and thick, extended outward and down to meet its powerful shoulders. From end to end, the mighty buck appeared twice the size of other deer. A hunter would brag that this deer was two hundred and fifty pounds, though the real weight might be under two hundred. The difference would most surely make for livelier conversation and bragging rights for the lucky one who bagged him, as if nature made such a creature for peculiar musings. But in nature, as in human life, to look bigger and stronger can make for less conflict, and the mere presence of the buck's shadow enabled him to ward off bloody battles for dominance with younger foes, which would ensure the longevity of the herd on Jenkins Mountain for many, many years to come.

It was uncharacteristic for him to be here, among the others of the first ledge, for this buck was out of place among all other deer. He was truly a deep mountain buck and his presence among the sunlit trees of the lower mountain was something of a freakish occurrence. The sun's rays bore witness to a creature like no other, possessed by the fever for sexual indulgence wrapped in the arrogant assimilation of self in the transferal of the seed of greatness. The moon and the stars knew of the beast, as it was typical of it to move under the cover of darkness and forage along the rugged, damp forest floor of the upper ledges, deep among the sweeping limbs of spruce and rows of thorny cedars. The nocturnal conditioning of the buck and the deep back mountain cover provided it with a blanket of security that could not be afforded to him elsewhere, and the nutrients provided by a consistently fruitful supply of acorns over the last three fall seasons only served to complement an already genetically sublime work of nature.

His coat was darker than the tan hair exhibited by most deer, almost charcoal in color with touches of tan throughout, and this despite the rough, sweaty exterior of the face and neck, was smooth and gleaming, capturing the warmth of the sun's rays. His underbelly was white as snow, full and rich, and left little doubt that this buck ate his fill even during the heart of the rutting season when many bucks go without food and rest. Between the rich, thick coat and the tight sheathes that encapsulated each powerful muscle of the beast were the surplus fat stores that supplied him the necessary energy for his unrelenting pursuits and conquests, wherever they might lead, as well as the bulkiness to help thwart any challenge to the throne of dominance. His eyes were big as plums and shined black under the protection of long black eye lashes. Pulsating blood vessels ran the length of his snout. They ran like winding, full-flowing rivers from his eyes on down to the white ripple around his wet, black nose. Nostrils flared with each pulsating vessel, and then relaxed ever so briefly before flaring again, exposing the pink lining of his nostrils.

His neck settled into two powerful shoulders, each a well-rounded center of mass, strong and well-endowed for its purpose; to carry the hefty weight of the neck and head of a king upon it. As he stood out in the clearing of the woods, the light gazing down through the trees sent shadows over his rippling shoulder muscles. His hair was darkest here, and it shined, enhancing the boundaries of the shoulder as it sloped into the muscles of his chest and rib cage. Upon his right shoulder and at its center was a small tuft of hair that stuck out beyond the rest, and under it was a deep, hollow depression that was bare right down to the white of skin. It was the size of a nail head in diameter, and it was the result of a hunter's bullet that had pierced him squarely when he was a mere six-point, year-and-a-half-old buck.

It had been a narrow escape for the then young six-pointer, as he was unaccustomed to the lure that his mighty head had on those who challenged the depths of the deepest and highest points of Jenkins Mountain. The young one had been pushed out of a pocket of spruce and rhododendron by his father, himself a twelve-point monster.

In rut and ready for romance, he kicked out all other bucks and patrolled the two-and-a-half square mile territory with all the grace of a half-crazed grizzly bear in search of ripe and ready does. Confused, and with no place to call home, the young offspring stood out like a sore thumb amongst a pocket of white birch, just south of the deep cover from which he was born and accustomed to. It was here on a clear November afternoon that a half-drunk city slicker on a two-day getaway from work, wife, and whore bore down the barrel of a brand new Winchester and took aim. Aiming for a neck shot, it was low and hit the buck in the tough, meaty shoulder muscle. Immediately upon impact, the young buck darted off with all the power it could muster from his three good legs. He ran southwest toward a deer run along the face of the cliff of the high ledge. The slicker, realizing his shot was off its mark, made ready for a second shot by moving into a clearing where he could get a better view of the running buck, all the while stumbling over fallen branches, rocks, and dense mountain floor cover. Once at the rocky cliff the buck, wounded and bleeding profusely, slowed down to a trot and limped on down through the narrow, steep path, his shoulder and right front quarters stiffening as he hopped on down the trail. He hobbled along over the jagged, rocky outcroppings, working his way quickly yet methodically further away from his pursuer.

By the time the slicker got to the ledge, he stumbled over to the edge and peered down at the winding path to find the wounded buck moving at a trotters pace halfway down the face of the rock. The fat man raised his gun to his shoulder and with one arm wiped the sweat from his eyes and zeroed in on his trophy. Instinctively he took one step forward to plant his lead foot before shooting, but miscalculated the distance to the edge. He stepped into a hole covered with leaves and twisted his knee. Trying in vain to catch his balance, the city slicker turned his torso and snapped his knee in two, falling as he did so eighty feet down, bouncing off the rocky face of the cliff as he went. Meeting his death before he hit bottom, his body was found two weeks later by another hunter. One week after that, at the funeral in Rockaway, New York, his wife met a woman she did not recognize. When she asked the women how she knew her late husband, the woman replied, "I was that fat fuck's whore, and he still owes me money!"

Chapter 12

THE ATTRACTION OF the great buck makes men do things that are beyond their own capabilities. And for these so-called men of the woods, doom surely awaits them. The great buck is a cunning creature, but it is the lure of the great and mighty crown that keeps the hunters returning to the woods. The attraction is for the trophy rack that sits atop his forehead. The antlers of this buck glowed bone white from the hours of rubbing and ripping apart the bark of the many tree trunks of cedar, spruce, hickory, ash, and oak that grew deep in the heart of the mountain. Thick as ax handles at their base, the antlers grew out of his forehead high and proud, and swept outward and upward as if offering to cradle the heavens. They seemed to proclaim to all other inhabitants that the one that walks with this crown is king of the woods, invincible over all, and ruler of the land.

A hunter's dream was brought to reality, and the old man would be closer to it than he could have ever imagined. Even in his youth, with all the energy and fire for the thrill of the hunt, when neither the weather nor his own circumstance in life could keep him out of the woods, not even then did he think of a buck as massive and majestic as this creature. How could he? It was unimagineable. And now, only fifty feet away in the thorny swallows of brush that encompassed the outer edge of the blowdown, stood a buck for the ages, yet the old man did not see him. Instead his attention was focused on the thick of cedar and spruce some distance away where the white flag gently swished back and forth under the cover of green, working her way up the next ledge.

How alive the woods now became, and how rusty and old the hunter now looked in contrast. Nature is not kind to old age, and this mountain and its inhabitants showed no mercy. The hunter's senses were dull, his keen awareness had given way to disorientation and lack of focus. Pitiful and confused, dazed and fragile was the old man who trusted only in the flagging tail up on the rocky incline leading to the second ledge. Tired and worn, the rifle heavy in his hands, he was more a man for the ages more so than of the present. And as quickly as the beast had appeared unseen before him, glorious and statuesque in the thorny mast, he was gone. The woods knew what the old man did not. For in the wood where all was ageless, the old man lost the battle over time. Right there, standing amidst the birch staring at a young deer with the happy tail feasting on some low-lying greens, the old man aged. The hour was near and the air grew a bit chilly as the change, the season of change, drew closer.

The chance of a lifetime had passed the old man by, perhaps blown away for good with the breeze that had whipped up from the northwest. That the old man had been unwise to the whole affair could not possibly damage his conscience with fleeting confidence or disgust, the kind that weighs heavy on the heart in the form of fruitless anxiety over a missed opportunity. His only fault was the betrayal of his own senses, which should have enlightened him to the attraction up ahead and his ever so slight movements amongst the ground cover. The doe with the happy tail continued on up through the cedars and spruce and eventually disappeared on top of the second ledge of the mountain. The rest of the afternoon proved to be uneventful, and as the day turned into dusk, the old man desired nothing more than to get his tired bones off the mountain and back to the truck, and put an end to the first day of the hunt.

Chapter 13

THEY WOULD ALL be out in front of the Main Street movie theater by now. When dusk came over the town, the townsfolk would all come out to see the spectacle. Every November, after the opening day of deer season was complete, the town held one of the biggest, most exciting events of the year, The Harvest Moon Festival. Mothers brought their children into town and retired folks with nothing better to do but gossip, get haircuts, and go to church, would be there too. Half the town parked curbside up and down Main Street to see them come strolling up to the Main Street movie theater in their jalopies and pickup trucks, some in fancy ragtops and metallic Thunderbirds and Buicks. They'd all be there with one thing in common, to show off their deer out in front of the Main Street Movie theater.

The hunters poured onto Main Street like soldiers come home from war. One after another the autos with deer on the roof, or on the hood, or in the trunk with the head hanging half out the back. Hunting parties squealed around Maple and onto Main in droves, pickup trucks with four men in the cab and another six sitting side by side on the outer edge of the wagon and ten bucks stacked up like firewood in the back, the red coats all huddled round them as they drove on down the street. The Main Street Diner was right next door to the movie theater, and they set up street-side and served coffee, hot tea, and cocoa for a nickel. The movie theater closed down for the evening, as the owner and operator was also a hunter. A sign in the theater window read, "Gone hunting, be back soon." For one evening in November, the town came together to celebrate the first day of deer season under the guise of the Harvest Moon Festival. They came to see the big bucks and find out if their friend or neighbor had been lucky enough to bag one of them. They came to hear the stories, often exaggerated, as well as the tales told for the very first time by the very men who concocted them.

The old man knew they would all be there. The new generation of hunters along with their families would all be there. Many of his friends and hunting buddies were dead or in retirement homes with the exception of Tony Canistro, but he thought that Tony's son would probably drive him into town for the great event, and he pondered the idea of driving in also before writing the day officially off the books. He reminisced of those years past when he and Tony hunted together and then drove into town, often times with fine deer to present to the waiting townsfolk. The sounds and smells of such an evening, the ripe aroma of deer lure against the backdrop of a young woman passing by on the sidewalk wearing a sweet perfume, were so distinctive in his mind that it made him uneasy. And the chatter; *ahh yes,* he thought, *the chatter from the sidewalk ....*

"Whose truck is that, anyways? Is that Billy Keagan's truck that just went by?"

The chatter was never-ending and started many a vicious rumor. "That's Billy's father's truck!"

The townsfolk set their calendars to such an event as this.

"Ray Keagan, does he still hunt?"

Blacks and whites, republicans and democrats, taxpayers and tax collectors, drunks and gamblers, preachers and housewives all came out to witness the hunters return from opening day.

"Billy's dad couldn't make it on account he's been hittin' the bottle a lot lately."

"Really? I didn't know he drank."

From high up above the apple farm, the old man, if he thought about it, could hear all the chatter, smell all the smells of Main Street, and see all the smiling faces that he remembered from his youth. It had all been tucked away deep in the recesses of his mind, and now it was all coming to him once again.

He remembered how much fun it really was. He and Tony in the middle of their season, so full of life, each with a family of his own, and yet they still snuck out to the woods on opening day and that evening they met their families in town at the Harvest Moon Festival to share the thrills, and many times, successes of the day.

And even those who were not fortunate enough to see or take the bounty of the deer came out and took part in the big event in town. They mixed right in with all the other red coats and drank coffee and hot chocolate and swapped stories with the victorious. For it was theirs as much as anyone's, and if they were in the woods on opening day, then no matter what their track in life before that day or after was not important. This was their time to share in the streetlight glare of a crisp autumn evening. It was like being part of a ball club in that if you wore the uniform, you were part of that special fraternity. The uniform was a red wool coat and pants and the special bond they shared was being one with the fraternity of hunters, and from that day and evermore they would remember the hunt.

Chapter 14

THERE WAS THE triumphant and the defeated, those polar opposites that caused elation as well as despair. It was for anyone and everyone. The less fortunate looked upon the lucky hunters standing next to their trophy bucks at the end of opening day. But most of those who fell short had many more opportunities to hunt another day and better the lucky ones with a skillful and daring hunt.

For Elmer, this would have been true years ago, but now he felt like the old man that he was. He walked slow and careful along the Jenkins Pass trail down the mountain to the orchard below. It was dark by the time he reached the opening of the top of Jenkins' apple farm. Far off in the distance, at the bottom of the long sweeping hill, a light beckoned. It was the porch light just off the back door of Jenkins' kitchen. It warmed the old man's bones just to get a glimpse of it and smell the chimney smoke, like a delicate hickory musk rising up from the valley. It was a sight and smell he accustomed himself to a thousand times when coming off of Jenkins Mountain at the end of a long day and out into the open fields overlooking the valley below. It always warmed him after a long day's hunt when he was cold and hungry.

As a boy, walking out of the woods with his father and older brothers, the light came from a kerosene lantern that hung from a crossbar just off the back porch of the kitchen. But then about twenty or so years ago, maybe more than that, the old man thought, the back porch was wired and the light, still in the same spot on the cross bar, beckoned him still. But the light looked the same from far up on the hill, and it made him feel young again. It made him feel like calling to his father the way he used to as a boy,

"Come out of the woods, Pa. Come out of the woods so we can go home and get what Ma's cooked up for us."

The light always seemed to signal the finish line, the end of a long day in the woods, the completion of a hard and worthwhile journey. It signified warmth, and going home again. Back then, Violet would have stew meat cooking in the black cast iron pot with lots of veggies, potatoes, gravy, and the old man's favorite, dumplings. Rose, their oldest child, would be mixing up a batch of dumplings while the other two played jacks under the kitchen table. When they heard the heavy boots coming up the steps of the back porch, the kids ran for the kitchen door to greet Daddy while Violet put the dumplings in the pot. He stared deep into the light at the bottom of the hill. It was all so long ago. Those he had loved were gone.

"Is it really home if the house is empty?" he asked.

A single brittle leaf on an apple tree rattled in a gentle breeze. The old man listened to it as he walked by.

Chapter 15

AS HE LAID his rifle across the front seat of the truck, the old man heard Ol' Gray the plow horse whinny. It was slight and distant, but he heard it and believed the horse must be getting ready to bed down in the barn for the night.

"What a day," muttered the old man with a sigh of tired frustration as he hopped up into the cab and slammed the door shut. He turned the key in the ignition, pulled the knob on the dash, and the headlights came on. While the engine fought to clear itself of the cold with coughs and wheezes, the old man pumped the gas pedal until finally the engine broke through with a loud, clear rumble that echoed across the valley. The old man sat back in the seat with his hands gripping the wheel, but he was in no rush to move. *It's good to sit on something soft again,* he thought,

"My butt has had quite enough of those rocks and tree trunks. I sure would like to know who was doing that shooting down near the beaver pond this morning. Maybe I should go into town right quick and investigate."

He pulled the pocket watch from his coat and held it close to the dash that had illuminated just enough for him to read the time if he squinted hard enough.

"Almost five," he said. "Yep, I think I'll go into town right quick."

Chapter 16

MAIN STREET WAS all aglow with the street lamps, the store fronts, and the traffic, which was mostly coming but some going. Main Street was busy but three times a year; Christmas Eve day, the Fourth of July, and the Harvest Moon Festival. *It never looked this busy,* the old man thought, as the truck crossed over Main and continued on down Maple. A parking spot was found curbside not even a block away from Main and the old man threw it in head first, killing the lights and the engine as he did so. The truck coasted in, the front end coming to a sudden screeching halt just inches from hitting the shined up chrome bumper of a brand new '54 Buick Roadmaster. The Buick's proud owner was Mayor Tom Delaney. Mayor Tom, as he was accustomed to being called, was an average-sized man, soft in appearance, with dark hair parted to one side, and a perfectly manicured face with no chin. He wore a business suit and tie tight to the Adam's apple on all occasions, whether business or festive. He had parked only minutes before and was on his way, with his wife Libby, to the festivities in the center of town. After escorting her from the passenger seat, he closed the door gently and methodically rubbed the ridge of the door with the cuff of his coat, not wanting to leave any smudges of fingerprints on the cream-colored finish. The couple stepped to the sidewalk and before making their way had stopped to admire the shiny new set of wheels, sparkling from the street lamp that it was parked under, and not just by coincidence. It was a proud moment that was quickly swept away and instantly replaced with fear and utter disbelief as the old man's truck rumbled recklessly up to the curb. When the truck's lights went out, Mrs. Delaney shrieked,

"Oh my god, Tom, that thing's gonna …!"

But she ran out of words in mid-sentence. Mayor Tom's jaw fell wide open and his soft, puffy face drew ghostly white until it practically glowed against the night.

"My god, oh my god, my car, no, no," he whimpered unintelligibly, until he finally let it all out loud and clear, "Sweet Jesus, what the hell do you think you're doin'?"

He crouched down to the curb and peered in at the crack of space between his shiny chrome bumper and the rusty iron cage that was the front of the old man's truck. A silver dollar could fit and hold between the two bumpers, and Mayor Tom was both enraged and utterly amazed all in the same breath. He stood and motioned as if ready to walk out from the curb and over the two cars to have a strong word with the driver of the truck, but stopped short, realizing that common sense said that he better walk around behind the truck, and so that is what he did. The driver's door opened and Mayor Tom was already there to greet the driver.

"What's the big idea," Mayor Tom shouted.

He then realized who the driver was and his tone quickly changed to a softer more subtle voice. "Oh Elmer, hello, I ah, didn't recognize your truck there. So you ah still drive, do ya?"

The old man didn't appreciate the question and so chose not to answer, but instead had a question of his own.

"What's ah matter, Mayor? You afraid my truck was gonna take your girl's virginity?" He pointed over to Mayor Tom's shiny new Buick.

"Uhh, Elmer, you remember Libby?" Mayor Tom asked anxiously as he motioned to the sidewalk, trying hard to save each one of them some degree of embarrassment.

"Oh, hello Libby, I didn't see you standing there," the old man said with not an ounce of indignity.

"What, did you lose weight?" he continued. "You're 'bout as skinny as that lamp post!"

With that, Mayor Tom almost swallowed his chin and poor Libby wanted nothing more than to crawl into her purse and hide.

The old man had a way with people that was all his own, and good or bad, it could only be said that it was all his own. Violet used to keep him from speaking his mind so freely. A simple cough or an elbow to the ribs was usually sufficient to put a lid on any thought or idea that was in his head from escaping through the mouth. Her greatness was that she knew her man so well that she could almost always read his mind or catch the look on his face that meant that a hot line was getting ready to escape. Then came the jab, and the line would remain untapped, never to hit the air. Without Violet around, the old man was as dangerous around words as firecrackers were around children. When they were lit, there was no telling what might happen.

The three walked together up Maple and onto Main.

"There's gonna be quite a crowd here this year," boasted Mayor Tom. "We got most of the shopkeepers going street-side this year. Yup, it's a little different than when we used to bring our deer into town."

Mayor Tom used to deer hunt but gave it up a couple of years after becoming mayor. He claimed that because of chronic lower back problems, he could no longer take to the woods, but many believed that he was afraid of being assassinated by an old political foe or an unhappy constituent. In any case, the mayor suffered from many ailments, such as paranoia and anal retention, but no one in town believed that back pain was one of them. Mayor Tom was in his fourth year and second term as mayor, and the old man thought him to be a crooked mayor and a lousy deer hunter.

"Ya know, Mayor, I don't recall you ever bringin' any deer to town," replied the old man, as he gave a subtle wink to Libby.

"Well anyway," Mayor Tom continued, waving his arms as he rambled on, "we got Marty the butcher doin' the sausage and peppers, and Joey Deval's got the rollaway bar set up, complete with his special deer hunters punch."

The name Deval was short for Devalentino, and Joe was the owner and bartender of Devalentino's Pub. The old man couldn't be altogether sure, but knowing Joe "D," the special punch that Mayor Tom referred to would most likely be one hundred proof grain alcohol mixed with any number of fruits, juices, and liquors.

"Lets see here," Mayor Tom continued. "Oh, we got Father Peter from Saint Augustine's opening up with a prayer, and he's also doin' a fifty-fifty raffle to support the holiday food drive. We also have Reverend Stephen of the First Presbyterian getting a piece of the action. Gotta keep them boys happy; ya know how it is. Anyway, Sprague's Hardware is gonna do a clearance sale just for the evening on some Farmall tractor accessories, and he's also got a hanging scale so we can weigh everyone's kill. And uhh, Pete Collasandra's gonna put out a baked goods display; ya know, like cannolis and apple turnovers, and ah he's even agreed to make the rolls for the sausage and peppers, so we got that covered!"

The old man thought of Mayor Tom as no more than a shady salesman at a used car dealership, which is what he owned before he became mayor, but he did know how to bring people together for a party. If being a politician was a talent and bringing people together was what politicians did, then the old man guessed that Mayor Tom had a talent. The whole town was really getting into the Harvest Moon Festival, and so he had to give Mayor Tom at least some credit.

"We got the Daughters of the American Revolution to sing 'God Bless America,' and uh they'll be backed up by Vince the barber and his barbershop quartet."

That Vince the barber, a Sicilian with the thickest of Italian accents straight off the boat a decade earlier, had put together a barbershop quartet, which to the old man was the corniest idea yet and he knew it must have come from the brain of Mayor Tom. The old man gave Mayor

Tom a raised eyebrow and slowly shook his head in utter disbelief. Upon seeing his reaction, Mayor Tom simply said, "Yeah, that was my idea too. Thought it would be a nice touch."

"Well, Mayor," the old man said, as he took off his hunting cap and slapped it on his pant leg, "looks like you've put together a real humdinger of a fireworks display that we're all gonna be walkin' into. We got plenty of guns, booze, old women, and a guinea leading us in a sing-a-long! Yep, you really outdid yourself this year, Mayor."

Mayor Tom caught the old man's sarcasm squarely, but he was so excited and full of himself that it had little effect on his mood, and he continued rambling on about the evening at hand.

A big crowd was gathering in the center of town and one side street was closed off to traffic to accommodate them. Sprague's Hardware Store was to the left of the Main Street movie theater and the town diner was to the right. Ed Sprague had his Farmall tractor equipment lined up and tagged right on the sidewalk with a sign that read, "One day clearance sale," and there was the hanging meat scale that was set up and in place just to the left of the movie theater, just like Mayor Tom said it would be. Directly in front of the theater was a three foot tall square podium. Erected just for the occasion, it was big enough to fit the barbershop quartet, half the Daughters of the American Revolution, and of course Mayor Tom. It was skirted in red, white, and blue on all sides and was equipped with a microphone and a music stand. As the hunters drove through town sporting their kill, a county conservation officer registered each head.

Those who had trophy kill unloaded their bucks on the sidewalk so the racks could be measured and the carcasses weighed. Those who didn't have trophy kill could also get their deer weighed, but most did not and kept driving on past.

About halfway up Main, the most recognizable used car salesman pulled his hands from the confines of his warm pockets and with Libby on his arm, set to work sniffing up to anyone of voting age. With one hand extended in the shaking position, they infiltrated a small street gathering and disappeared into the middle of it. Happy to rid himself of the Mayor's company, the old man continued on up the busy sidewalk.

The town came pouring in from side streets, storefronts, and the inside of parked cars. Hunters drove up Main slowly, beeping their horns and yelling out to those they knew on the sidewalk. Some of the hunters were sporting sizeable kill on the trunks of their cars and trucks, and some of them had them tied across the front hood or even the roof. A hunting party drove up in a red Ford pickup with two hunters in the cab and another four sitting on the flatbed with five good-sized bucks in between them, the heads practically hanging off the back bumper. The hunters in the cab were older than the ones on the flatbed, but the old man did not recognize any of them. The ones on the flatbed were young men, practically boys. They laughed and joked with each other and waved to the folks on the sidewalk. They appeared to be having a very good time, and it was obvious that they had made the most of their day in the woods.

As he continued walking up toward the movie theater, watching the cars for people he might know, the old man caught a whiff of the sausage and peppers Marty the butcher had cooking and could see smoke filling the air up ahead. Marty had carved up many a deer for the old man over the years. His prices were always reasonable, and he knew what cuts of venison would make the best roasts and chops. But his true genius as a butcher was how he prepared the ground venison for sausages and meatballs. The sausages were the hottest and tastiest in the county, prepared with just the right amount of ground pork and Italian seasonings and lots of red pepper, and the meatballs, when simmered in a nice red wine and tomato sauce for an entire afternoon, melted in your mouth. When Violet cooked up spaghetti and meatballs for a Sunday dinner in November or December, Elmer couldn't wait to get home to the dinner table.

As he got closer to Marty's street-side setup just outside the butcher shop, the old man's stomach let out a growl from under the heavy red coat that was heard by a couple of young girls walking alongside of him. They giggled when they heard the sounds emanating from his midsection, and he put his hand up to his belly, just slightly embarrassed. He had not eaten since before noontime, and the smells of peppers and onions being sautéed in red wine was more than he could bear. For a brief time the old man completely forgot about hunting and who was shooting below him on the mountain. All his thoughts and actions were controlled by his stomach and the sweet smells of pork fat and mesquite drippings burning off in the fire pit up ahead. The old man pushed his way through the crowd and up to Marty's stand.

"Hey Elmer, how you been?" Marty yelled out with a big smile when he saw the old man.

"I was just talkin' about you with some guys I know, just a couple a days ago."

"I'm doing good, Marty, and how about yourself?" asked the old man as he shook Marty's thick, greasy hand.

Marty stood six feet two inches tall and weighed well over two hundred and fifty pounds. Every ounce of him was built the traditional Italian way—eating, eating, and more eating. He was big and barrel-chested with thick forearms and pudgy fingers that connected to a hand that some people might have mistaken for a bear paw. He could drink, and was known to put back more than a few with the boys when he was younger. Nowadays it was a bottle of red wine every evening with the traditional Italian supper. He was pushing sixty but could still do mop up duty on anyone who showed disrespect to him or his friends. Some said he was connected with some people from down in the city, but the old man didn't know much about that and didn't want to know.

"So you were talking about me," the old man said with a smile. "Only good things I hope?"

"Of course only good things," Marty insisted as he took his hand back and using a long metal spoon stirred the peppers and onions that were being sautéed in a big, black cast iron fry pan.

"I was talkin' with some fellas I know down in the city and they was askin' who the best hunter and tracker was up here in these parts and I told them that you were the best that I could think of. But then I was thinkin' that you had given up this game 'cause I haven't seen you in a real long time."

Marty took a gallon-sized jug of table wine from his

work station, pulled the cork, and poured some of the wine over the peppers and onions, causing them to be engulfed in steam. He then took a long two-pronged fork with a wooden handle and flipped some sausages that were on a grill over an open flame. The flame came from a fifty-gallon tin drum that was cut in half from top to bottom and put up waist level on two sawhorses. The half-cut drum was filled with wood that was sprayed down with mesquite oil before it was set on fire, and after the wood had burned down to the hot coals, a large square grill was set on top of the drum. A lot of heat was generated from the drum, and Marty stood over it in nothing more than a long sleeve button-down red, white, and black checkered shirt with the sleeves rolled up to the elbows, exposing his massive forearms, and the front unbuttoned from just above the belly, revealing his gray-haired, barreled chest.

"They needed a guy for some job, and I was gonna give 'em your name, but didn't think you'd be up for it."

Marty was trying to say in a nice way that he thought Elmer was too old to still be hunting but didn't know how to say it. The old man caught Marty's gist.

"Just as well," declared the old man, "'cause I don't want to be some guide for anyone, much less some bums from down in the city."

Marty wasn't offended, for he had known the old man for far too long and knew that he wouldn't intentionally insult any of his friends.

"Hey," said Marty, quick to change the subject, "remember that nitwit who was killed a few years back up on Jenkins Mountain?"

Yes, I remember," answered the old man. "I guess that guy could've used a guide, what do ya think?"

Marty laughed and nodded his head in agreement. "I think you're probably right on that one!"

Marty took the sausages from the grill and mixed them in with the peppers and onions and added more wine from the jug. The old man watched as he mixed them together, the smells filling all of Main Street. When he was finished, he took a long Italian roll, pulled it apart with his bear-like hands, planted two hot sausage links in it, and then smothered it in the sautéed peppers and onions. He folded the sandwich in a white paper plate and handed it to the old man.

"So how was your day?" he asked, as he waved off the two dollars that the old man had pulled out of his coat pocket.

"Not too good," the old man said in an unfortunate tone of voice.

"Where did you go?" asked Marty.

"I walked Jenkins Mountain," answered the old man.

"Jenkins Mountain! You walked Jenkins Mountain?" asked Marty, who was more than just a little surprised by the answer.

"Well, only the first ledge," answered the old man.

"You mean you were hunting from a stand on the edge of the orchard?" Marty asked thinking that the old man must have been mistaken.

"No," the old man said matter-of-factly. "I spent most of my day walking the first ledge and saw nothing.

"Wow!" Marty exclaimed, thoroughly impressed. "Well, I guess you're in better shape than I thought."

Marty thought for a moment, remembering what he wanted to tell the old man.

"You know who got a big buck today?"

"Who?" The old man asked grudgingly, unsure that he wanted to hear the answer.

"Joe Styles shot at least a ten-pointer, and I thought someone said he got him up on Jenkins Mountain."

The old man had only taken two or three bites from his sausage and pepper sandwich, but he could feel his appetite slowly fade away. The hot and sweet flavors of the sausage mixed with the peppers and onions that made his taste buds come alive in an explosion of flavor quickly disappeared and all that he could taste was the bile that had lined his empty stomach only minutes before.

"Well, I gotta get goin'," the old man said to Marty with a wave. "Good to see ya, and if I get my deer, you'll be seeing me again."

"Okay," Marty said, as he shoveled sausage and peppers into rolls for the many patrons who had lined up along his grill, "I'll be seein' ya, Elmer, and good luck!!"

Holding the sandwich in his hand folded in the white paper plate, the old man walked further up the street until he came to the Main Street movie theater. A big crowd had gathered here and many of the hunters had parked their cars right next to the theater so they could haul their deer off the cars and into line to be tagged, measured, and weighed.

Joe Styles was the one time no-good son-in-law of Tony Canistro. He had a past, and none of it good. He was a local deli owner who ran a sit-down counter on the north end of town. After many a morning's hunt, the two men would go to Joe's place for a quick bite to eat and a chance to warm up before returning to the woods. Tony respected Joe for his entrepreneurial spirit, and so he introduced him to his daughter. The two were married and divorced within a year. Joe, as it turned out, was mixed up with a gang of racketeers out of New York along with some younger folks in town. There were never any serious stories to tell about Joe, but the more one got to know him, the more he appeared to have slime on his hands. The old man knew him as Slimey Joe. It was a bitter pill to think that Joe was the one in the woods doing all that shooting, but at the same time it made sense.

The Daughters were singing "God Bless America" and Mayor Tom was doing his best impersonation of an honest, upstanding citizen of the community, just one of the people. He stood to the right of the old ladies on the podium, and with his wife still hand-locked at his side, sung the words as best he could remember them. His voice, loud and out of sync, echoed through the crowd, burying the voices of the women, who appeared to be more than a little irritated. Many in the crowd sung along as they filed past the viewing area where the biggest bucks were being weighed and measured. Each deer was tagged with the hunter's name and the territory where the deer was taken. The old man counted fifteen bucks tagged and registered. The bucks were nice sized, but one stood out amongst the others. It was a ten-pointer with a massive spread, each side a mirror image of the other, sweeping up and outward high off the head before bending toward each other at the tips.

The old man's heart sank, his breath grew slight, as if his soul had been taken from him, robbed by another who had no soul and no shame. The dreams he shared with no one but Tony and the Brittany lay dead before him at the hands of another. The buck that the Brittany jumped in the early October hunt, the one that had reinvented the old man's enthusiasm for the game and the spirit for adventure that was left for dead far behind on Jenkins Mountain many years before, had died again. It lay dead on the sidewalk with a swollen, colorless tongue hanging from its mouth, its insides ripped out, replaced only with a stick to keep its empty cavity open, and the old man felt as though he should lay down next to him also with a stick jammed up under his ribs.

Chapter 17

JOE STYLES HAD never killed any game creature in his life with only one shot. It was well known in town that he was a terrible shot and an even worse hunter. He could not sneak up on prey, for he walked with heavy, flat feet, and even for a relatively healthy young man, he walked clumsily and had extremely poor balance and coordination. He could not sit and post for he bored easily, and when his attention shifted his body grew spastic. He shifted in his seat and picked at his clothes or broke twigs with his hands, or scratched and poked at his body. And because of his shuffling gait and noisy approaches and lousy attention to detail, he could not track an animal outside of fifty yards from a post, be that animal alive or dead. Even worse than these less than admirable traits was that Joe was oblivious to these shortcomings and even thought of himself as a rather fine deer hunter. Other strategies of hunting were never perfected because he never came to accept that any of his current methods were faulty. So when he felled a ten-point buck with a fourth and final shot on the lower skirts of Jenkins Mountain, just north of the beaver pond, his only surprise was how big the animal was. He had missed the deer with three successive shots a little earlier that morning.

Joe had come up from the backside of the beaver pond just at first light from a property that neighbored Jenkins' farm. He walked a meadow trail to the pond and followed a deer run through the high reeds of a section of soggy swampland that wrapped around three-quarters of the pond. The reeds stood tall throughout much of the swamp, and Joe twice got confused as to what direction he was walking and had to turn back. If not for his sunken boot imprints in the mud, he would have been hard-pressed to find his way at all. The bog and swamp-filled reeds were much bigger and more extensive than the pond itself, and much of it was dry and hard enough for man or beast to walk through without sinking in too deep. Just as he made his way to the outer edge of the high reeds bordering the first of the wooded ledges of the mountain, Joe jumped the buck with four does. As the surprised deer flagged off their white tails with long-legged leaps over downed birch trees and other outer swamp foliage, Joe swung his rifle around from his shoulder harness and shot wildly, not aiming or knowing what to aim at. His heart pounded heavy. Arms and legs jolted with uncoordinated spastic energy. Joe's upper lip quivered as he discharged his weapon, *Boom! Boom! Boom!* The deer stayed together and ran north up the first ledge. They ran hard until the buck caught wind of another scent from further up the hill. It was the scent of a man, possibly another hunter, still some distance away, but the scent carried with the breeze and the buck turned back. The does caught the scent too but continued on, as if assuming the role of protector for the buck, like obedient soldiers they would carry on into harm's way so that the young prince might escape a terrible fate. The four does continued on in the direction from where the scent was coming and then angled off as they got closer and trotted up in the direction of the second ledge of the mountain. The safety of the tall reeds of the swamp was all the buck knew, and only minutes after turning back to pick up one of the many trails that lead to the cover of the swamp, a hot steel barrel aimed in at the nape of his neck. The ten-pointer fell dead, never hearing the big boom of the gun. The one up on the hill with the man scent heard the final echoing boom as did the four does, and for each of them, all was lost as the boom cued up through the rocky ledges of the land.

Chapter 18

THE KING OF the woods came down off the high ledges that evening and fed in the apple orchard of the north field until early the next morning. The rut had exhausted him, as he had run the highest peak of Jenkins Mountain in search of the best candidates for mating and continued on through the lower ledges, mating every doe he could find and fighting any buck that even so much as looked in his general direction.

Although fighting to the death is not customary among whitetails, it does happen sometimes. Earlier on this day it proved fatal for one young buck that thought himself big enough to handle the king. The king had run wild from midnight to the wee morning hours of opening day. Through the rough country high ledges of the mountain he ran, and by first light had come down off the high ground to the first ledge. For some time he played a game of cat and mouse through the dense fog with a doe in estrus, another younger buck who was attracted to the same doe, and an unwelcome intruder who was nestled in near a blown over tree. The salty, stale smell of the intruder gave him away. The smaller buck was rightful heir to the throne, not just by brute, but also by blood, should anything happen to the king. The king came up the hill of the first ledge, walking with the fog and smelling the rich morning air as he did so. The big buck was cautious, the intruder rusty, and the future heir hungry for a mate and ready for a fight. Caught in the fog by the eye of the intruder, the king should have been shot as a terrific trophy, a prize that would have made a hunter's life complete. But the veil of fog hid the big buck, and the intruder missed his chance. In a brief instant the king vanished, leaving the floating fog to solidify the fate of the younger buck in the blowdown where the king was now headed. The king moved slowly and quietly deep into the heart of the blowdown and began circling the doe he intended to make his.

The doe, whose attention without need for affection was in such high demand, stood still in a thorny mast at the center of the broad, reclusive blowdown. Limbs of cedar and spruce were cast so tight and strewn about in such haphazard fashion that the king, only several feet away from his subject, could not see her but could only smell her ripe scent. The younger buck made his way into the blowdown from its northernmost entrance, a skinny deer trail that skirted along its borders with thick, thorny wild rosebushes, its vines strung out over the trail. As the damp mountain air filtered up through the thick of the forest with the fog, the king caught wind of the younger buck and set himself to the task of intercepting and destroying him. With his head low to the ground and his black, plum-sized eyes opened wide, he slowly moved into position in a heavily guarded enclave of thorns and half-blown over cedars that cut off any advance the younger buck could make at the doe.

The heart of the king pounded away, a divine fury

boiled and pulsated through his veins, causing a putrid odor to emanate from the pores of his skin and run like water out and over his dark coat. No longer able to control his immense physique from the boost of hot-tempered blood that ran through his core, the king thrust his massive head from side to side, keeping his rack low to the ground. *Swoosh! Swoosh!* His head swept the floor of the forest, catching, shaking, and ripping apart the tough, wild vines and thorny rosebushes. Again and again he did this, catching the thorny bushes and hanging wild vines in his rack. He ripped them up as if they had no roots at all to hold them in the earth and shook and tangled them in his rack, and with a shake from his powerful neck he cast them all about. The sounds from the middle of the blowdown were of anger. The thorny vines of the wild rosebushes stabbed and scratched his nose and ears, this their only defense against the raging monster, but their ripping and tearing open of deer flesh only lent to more aggression, and as the trickles of blood began to run down the face and neck of the beast, the sounds of the forest being ripped apart only grew more intense.

The commotion in the forest so close to her did not cause the doe to seek refuge elsewhere. She didn't scare easily, for her natural instincts and biological intuitions told her that this was all somehow part of the plan, but she may have been a bit alarmed as to the enormity of the commotion, and so she stayed frozen in the seclusion of cedar and thorny mast. The younger buck was neither scared nor alarmed at the ruckus and deemed himself perfectly capable and ready to trade scare tactics and even physical torture if necessary. The stage was set and the motives clear for all those involved with the exception of the intruder, who stood with his rifle in hand far enough away from sight and sound through the dense forest cover and early morning fog. The younger buck moved cautiously, sniffing the cool, wet air and twitching his ears back and forth as if to gather more evidence as to the size and whereabouts of his opponent. The thrashing of brush and vines intensified, and the younger buck continued on toward it. The early morning rains came and went and then came again in the form of a fine mist, making silent all creatures traveling afoot, and yet the young buck moved carefully, each step touching down lightly on the soggy forest floor. He moved as an army of one, confident but cautious, inquisitive yet methodical in his approach. Onward through the depths of the blowdown where the sounds of violence could no longer be even remotely contained but now had become the audible fury of the possessed. It broke, it crackled, and it shook with echoes of grunts and heavy breathing. And as the young buck made his last advance before coming into view of the king, the noise ceased and an eerie silence fell upon the woods. The gentle spray continued and a patch of dense fog infiltrated through the tiniest of openings in the fortress that was the blowdown. When a break in the fog came, the king was gone. No blue jay or roosting turkey or family of squirrels gave his movements away and the leaves would not betray him, at least not in the hour at hand. The ears of the young buck twitched and his nose sniffed the cool morning air, but these devices, although good, were not good enough to save him. The charge came from his right flank with such force that his midsection became sandwiched between the massive horns of the king and a vine-entangled hickory tree.

The horns pierced his side. The weight of the aggressor snapped the ribs of the young deer. They cracked and popped outward like knives piercing his inner flesh. The king forced his horns this way and that, causing the jagged broken pieces of rib bone to rip and shred the outer walls of the younger buck's midsection. The king had pushed hard into the side of the wounded one, trapping him against the thick forest cover. The king's neck and shoulders stiffened, crushing the younger buck. The smaller buck gave way, pushing his wounded body through the dense entanglement of vines and thorny mast only to get caught in the vast web that was the blowdown. The king followed in a relentless pursuit. When it was over, the young one lay dying.

The king pulled away and stood over his own offspring. The young one had been outmaneuvered in the chess match of the woods, outwitted by a foe greater and nastier than any in his habitat. The king had killed one of his own in an attempt to continue the mating ritual. It was a small price to pay for dominance. It was a small price to pay for the unfettered continuance of mating. The king stood over his fallen son, too weak and exhausted to move, half in a trance, not in the right mind to even understand what he did and why he did it. After a long while had passed, he moved sluggishly through the high, dense thorny bushes toward the doe he sought. But he was too late; when he got to the spot in the thorny bushes where the doe had been earlier in the morning, he found only her scent. He followed her trail through to the outer edges of the blowdown, but could muster no more energy to continue the chase. The king watched from the very edge of the blowdown as the doe made her way up the hill to some cedars. His head stuck out into the open woods but his body would move no further, and as the doe made her way up the hill to the crest of the next ledge, the almighty buck slowly sunk back into the fortress of the blowdown and collapsed, too weak to go on.

In the wild the dangers are many and uncertainty lies just beyond the reaches of any hill, ledge, or tree line. With this uncertainty are the unkindest cuts of savagery and sacrifice. For the king, the destiny that was his would be determined on some other day, perhaps on some other hill. His exhaustion saved him from the barrel of the gun and the hunter who owned it.

A slight breeze tickled a shriveled leaf on a wild grapevine. When it could cling no more, it fluttered and spun to the earth and lay beside the fallen young buck to become part of the forest floor.

Chapter 19

BEFORE HEADING HOME, the old man decided it was time to pay someone a visit. It was long overdue. He was not looking forward to the showdown. At the corner of Main and Elm stood St. Augustine's Catholic Church. Elmer walked in, hat in hand. He was nervous. He didn't know if he should sit or stand. He stood. After some time had passed, he found the words.

"Hey old man, You're even older than me. I'm not sure what I want to say to Ya exactly, but I ah … well, I haven't been around in a long time. You took my inspiration … You know that, and well, I been a little busy being angry. Should it be me or You? Should I be mad at me or You for not doing more? Ya see, I loved her. I cared for her. I tried to keep her safe. When You took Danny, I tried …. But see that was a bad thing You did, taking our son. And she … well, it weighed hard on her. It weighed hard on me. I didn't know that her pain would turn into the cancer. I would have gladly taken her pain to keep the cancer from her, but see, You didn't give me that choice. I only asked You to keep my family safe … that You help me. I worked hard, I didn't complain. But I complain now. Why, why was I not given a choice, me for her?"

The old man put a fist into his cap and put the cap on his head.

"I don't know why I come to You now after all this time. All these years I've asked the question to myself, not having the stomach to ask You. I stayed away thinking it was all my fault, that maybe I caused all of it. But it wasn't my fault. I go to her grave every so often, and I tell her I'm sorry, hoping that she will tell me that it's okay. I miss her. I miss my family." The old man stood motionless with clinched fists, ready for a showdown. His eyes were tense on the cross in the front of the sanctuary.

After all the words spoken, all the emotions laid down on the altar of faith, the old man heard no response. He paused. Feeling rejected, he slowly turned and walked toward the door. It had been a long day. The old man decided it was time to go home.

Chapter 20

THE HOUSE WAS dark except for a patch of light from the porch lamp that shone through the kitchen window. The house was cold; the coals in the wood stove once hot had burned out early in the morning. It was a lonely old house in need of some repairs, but mostly in need of inhabitants who could give it life and color, warmth and light. There was a time when children ran through the house, giving its rooms and hallways laughter and a playful atmosphere filled with song and adolescent creativity. And where there were children, there were doting parents and loving husband and wife. It was a house that heard the babies cry, the children laugh, and the occasional family squabble. In the spring, the windows opened to fresh new days filled with hope and wonder, the hickory in the backyard, its many limbs ready to bud, and the crocuses at its base opening in the early morning hour. In the cool air just as the early evening broke, the deer came out of the woods to graze in the yard and the crickets and peepers were loudest at this time. The deer had not been seen for a long time. They grazed and played in the yard between the house and the brook that edged the wood line. And while the deer played and the newly thawed water of the brook trickled on through clear and cold, the family in the house sat down to dinner and gave thanks that they were a part of the beautiful spring. In late spring and early summer, while the father worked his garden and managed his property, his children fished the brook behind the house and played in the yard until their father gave them chores of their own. The summers were filled with picnics, American flags, vegetables from the garden, and long, hot evenings on the back porch drinking lemonade and watching the fireflies sputter about in the night against the backdrop of the moon and stars. And while Rose, the oldest daughter, dreamily set her eyes to the stars from her bedroom window, thinking of the boy of her dreams, the one she had not yet met, Danny, the oldest boy, sought the moon with dreams of becoming a great general like Washington or even Pershing, the great American hero he had read about that day in the newspaper. And so during the summers when the younger children slept, and the older ones dreamed, and their parents thought of days gone by, the deer of the woods grew big and ran the hills with passion and played in the yard under the blanket of night. The fall brought with it the chill in the early evening air and the rich red and orange colors painted upon the land. The grouse were plentiful in the fall, and good shots meant table meat dressed, covered in bacon, and stuffed. To complement the hunter's good fortune was the fall harvest of sweet potatoes, pumpkin, string beans, and beets that the children picked from the garden and Mother prepared in the kitchen for long hours while her young ones read to her and did their school work. The fall also meant Halloween tricks and treats, caramelized apples, and evil-looking hallowed out pumpkins on the front porch.

Games of hide and seek in a darkened house where ghools and goblins lurked only capped off an already terrifying and stimulating time for the young at heart. When the harvest came and the cold months began to set in, the kitchen became the warmest, friendliest, and most interesting place to be, and the aromatic flavors, spices, and seasonings filled every room, closet, and crawl space in the entire house. In years of prosperity, and these were few, the Christmas dinner would be a fattened pig bought from a local farm. The leftovers would mean meals for an entire month, with every last morsel of pork being used. In less prosperous times Christmas dinner would come from the hills of Jenkins Mountain—a venison rump roast or tenderloin—and the hunter who bagged the feast carved it with a pride that no king from any throne could afford. Christmas carols, hot apple cider, a neighborly pop-in to offer wishes, and warm fingers and toes at the fireplace were always anticipated. This house had seen it all through many seasons, year after year. The sounds, smells, and personalities resonated through its walls and up into the attic of memories where they lay quietly tucked away, unable to visit again, but not wanting to be forgotten.

Chapter 21

THROUGH THE KITCHEN door the old man walked, weary and achy with a cold that ran through the core of his body right to his bones. The Brittany was there to greet him, tail wagging with a stiff, awkward gait from sleeping in a ball on the floor all day.

"Hey Ol' Bohemian, how are you this evening? Did you hold down the fort while I was gone? I sure hope you did. You're a good ol' boy, now go out and do your business!"

Bo didn't mince visiting with his master but for an instant before running out the open door and into the cool night to relieve himself. A longer, more exhausting day the old man could not remember, as he threw the light switch and plopped himself down on a kitchen chair. The red cap that sat atop his balding head was carelessly flung onto the table, and a long sigh of frustration fluttered through his lips. With an elbow on the table, he ran his hand back and forth over his forehead, massaging it until he collected his thoughts. The Brittany barked at the kitchen door, and his master obediently answered by rising and opening the door.

"The temperature's gonna drop tonight, Ol' Bo. I

better fire up the wood stove before I undress. No point in freezin' my butt off."

With that he walked stiffly into the parlor and made ready to start a fire that would burn hot through the night.

As the old man, still in his long johns, relaxed in his lazy chair in front of the warm fire, a mug of hot coffee in his hand, he opened his hunting diary and scribbled some words from a poem he had been working on:

When the fall comes, think of me. I can be heard on any mountain seen in any town, and felt in any man who has a passion for living as his father lived, learning what he taught, and breathing the free, crisp, autumn air that he breathed . And so I climb the high mountain in search of the great buck, if only to get a glimpse of him and feel my heart skip a beat before it jumps out of my chest. The great buck I seek is king and keeper of the woods, just as I am the keeper of all that my father taught. And as I do all that I can to bring the great beast to my sight, I know that he is king and that it is I who am wounded, for time is fleeting, and my family is gone. The king is proud and runs hard with great, outstretched strides, that make him invisible between the trees. His loins have succeeded in carrying a bloodline of superiority to a land that will prosper whether he now lives or dies. But I will surely die and none of my seed will see what I see or live what I have lived. I have outlived my children and will return to my creator and search for all who I have loved. And so when the fall comes, think of me. I can be heard on any mountain, seen in any town, and felt in any man who has a passion for living as his father lived ....

He closed the journal and rested it on his lap. Putting his head back, he began to drift away into a dreamland where the great deer roamed. He dreamed he was back on Jenkins Mountain in the spot where he was posting that very day, but in his dream he did not fail to see the big, burley buck. The vision that stood before him in the woods was glorious, rich in color and detail, from the white on his neck to the tan and charcoal hair that made up his thick body. His massive horns stuck up high and proud through the fog, through the branches of hickory and birch and through the thick, thorny mast of the blowdown. The old man's eyes were good and his reflexes quick, just like when he was a kid. As the snow fell he stood over the dead king, the barrel of the rifle still smoking in the crisp morning air. The old man breathed in the smell of black powder until he awakened, disappointed that it was all just a dream.

He pushed his aching bones up from the lazy chair and made the slow, painful walk to the bedroom. Bo followed in the same manner; each suffered from muscles that were quick to cramp and stiffen and bones that creaked and ached on cold days from so many years of loyal service. The old man sighed as his head hit the pillow and was out before Bo finished his own ritual: four to five circles in place before taking his bed on the hardwood floor.

They dreamed of places and times gone by, of days when they were young and spry. Their dreams took them to the people and things that mattered most. Violet came to the old man and comforted him. She was young and beautiful again, with her whole life ahead of her. Her skin was soft and smooth again, unlike the way she looked when she had the cancer. Her blonde hair was long and shiny and the sunlight streamed through it and warmed him. She spoke to him in a voice that was clear and mesmerizing, yet it was barely above a whisper.

"Elmer, see the deer playing in the yard near the brook? Isn't it wonderful to be home again? Danny can't wait to see you. He says, 'Hi Daddy, hi Daddy.' Danny says the big deer is on the north side of the mountain and halfway home. Danny says, 'See you when you get home, Daddy, see you when you get home.'"

Violet came close to him and whispered in his ear, "Hurry up, Santa. I love you, Elmer."

The old man woke still thinking and hoping that Violet was with him, but she wasn't, and the reality of it all settled on him that it was just a dream. *It seemed so real*, he thought, and the words echoed in his ears. Everything seemed so vivid. No longer able to sleep, he leaned over and switched on the lamp on the nightstand and checked the time. The big hand eventually came into focus. It was two thirty. The old man got out of bed and lazily walked out of the room and down the hall to the kitchen.

"Got to make sure," he said to himself in a whisper. "Got to make sure this was all a dream."

He flipped on the light switch and grabbed a cup from the cupboard and filled it with cold tap water from the kitchen faucet. He took a long, cool drink. Leaning against the sink, he peered out the kitchen window and thought with a half-crazed expression of disbelief about his dream.

"Violet said Danny called me Daddy. He never called me Daddy 'cept for when he was just a little kid. Called me Dad the last time I ever saw him just before he shipped out to Pearl Harbor. God, for just a few minutes,

I thought I had my family with me again, just like it was years ago when we were all here at home, just starting out, our whole lives in front of us."

The walls were the only things left to answer his thoughts and questions. They creaked with the slightest breeze, expanded and contracted with the heat from the wood stove. But the old man could translate the sounds. He said no more and walked back down the hall to his room and tried to sleep, but sleep did not come easy, for the words and the vision of Violet consumed him. Her words lingered in the air with a cool draft and the slight smell of crocuses. Those were her favorite flower, and they came up out of the earth with the first sign of spring. But spring was still four months off, and the crocus bulbs lay dormant around the hickory trees in the backyard. Violet had planted them long before she gave birth to Danny. Every spring, just after the first thaw, they sprouted. The smell in the air caused him pain, just as the first thaw caused him pain, just as the crocuses sprouting beside the hickory trees caused him pain. After a long while, he fell into a deep sleep.

In the early morning hour, just before sunup, the phone let out one long ring from the post on the kitchen wall. The old man heard it and awoke, bewildered. It did not ring again. The echo filled his ears with an uneasy melody. Like a shock wave, the ring hung in the air. It was enough to get the old man out of bed to start his morning. He slept long enough, even if it was not well, and decided to dress and make ready for another day in the woods.

"I think I'll have a quick breakfast at Maude's," the

old man said, as he walked down the hall and into the kitchen to let Bo out.

Chapter 22

"COME ON IN, folks, we're a family establishment. Pick a booth. We got jukeboxes in every booth. Check 'em out! How 'bout a little Sinatra? Sinatra goes perfect with a piece ah apple pie and coffee. Bring your honey to Maude's soon as the movie lets out. We'll be seein' ya again real soon, maybe for breakfast. We're open at four."

"Shirley, I'll have some more coffee when ya getta chance! Where's ma eggs? Tell Oscar to burn the potatoes. Don't forget the toast now, Shirley."

"I only have two hands, Earl. You'll hafta wait!"

"Clear those plates, get 'm in and get 'm out."

"Where's my breakfast? Got things ta do and people ta see."

"Any room at the counter? How 'bout a booth; that'll work if there's no more room at the counter. That Shirley is one sweet-looking woman; big-chested and rose hips, would ya look at her! What did you just say? She's got two kids? Damn shame."

"Hey Blondie!"

"Name's Shirley; you know better than that, Fred. Hey Fred, ya think she's a real blonde?"

Maude's Diner was a greasy spoon, the only one in

town. It was right on Main Street and it catered to truck drivers and businessmen, hunters and politicians. Its doors opened at four AM and it was standing room only by six. Maude's appealed to the town. It was the town more than the town hall was the town. It was all here, the meeting place among steak and potatoes, eggs and bacon. Maude's was the rendezvous point for coffee and eats on the table and sensitive deals and shady enterprise under it. If you wanted to be seen, wanted the full story on someone, or the scoop on local events, you could find it between five and six in the morning at Maude's.

The specialty of the house was the corned beef hash and poached eggs, and if you treated Shirley the waitress with an ounce of decency and commented on her youthful appearance and firm ass, she might just throw you the toast on the house. If a man dared pinch her ass, he would be expected to ask the single forty-year-old mom of two out on a date. Shirley had not been out in years.

Most times, early in the morning before the day's hunt, Elmer and Tony would walk in together and sit at the counter. Over eggs and coffee they would discuss strategy but never over a whisper, as other hunters were known to eavesdrop and steal the best laid plans for a hunt.

"Those were the good ol' days," the old man thought as he walked through the glass door of Maude's Diner and straight up to the familiar surroundings of the counter.

Oscar gave a wave and a smile and the old man did the same as he took off his red hunting cap, placed it on the counter, and sat down.

The old man preferred the counter to the booth and a

T-bone steak with fried eggs instead of the house special. He liked the eggs sunny-side up with extra crispy refried potatoes, toast, and coffee. For him the toast was always on the house, even though no comments were ever made toward Shirley or her ass. Shirley just plain liked the old man, thought he was sweet. Oscar, the Mexican cook also liked him and usually waved from his post at the grill, as it was visible to the counter.

Shirley poured him a hot cup of coffee and the old man placed his order even though he didn't need to, as Shirley knew it by heart. The old man forgot the refried potatoes and Shirley had to remind him with a sarcastic smirk. Grateful that she remembered, he smiled and nodded.

"Thank you, Shirley. I think you know me better than I know myself."

He had not yet taken a sip of coffee when in with a gust of cold air he heard a familiar voice from behind him. It was Mayor Tom who came bustling through the front door all bundled up in his tan Woolworths overcoat. Even before the glass door had a chance to slam shut, Mayor Tom was off and running, shaking hands and saying his hellos.

"Hello, hello, good to see ya Al … and John. Good to see ya Carmine, and how is your wife feeling? Is she still under the weather? What did you think of that night last night? That was really something, wasn't it?"

It was a little early for such banter, and so the old man did not bother turning around to acknowledge him. But he knew he wouldn't need to. Mayor Tom hung up his coat and headed to the counter for a seat. He also wasn't one for the booth, for he enjoyed the openness of the counter. The patrons, the voters, could see him right out there eating with them and talking to them and helping the economy of the town.

"Hello Elmer, good to see you out nice and early. Looks like you're headed for another day in the woods. Lot ah nice deer taken yesterday, and how about that buck that Joe Styles shot, wasn't that something?"

The old man just nodded and grinned, the coffee cup to his mouth hid his frustration.

"Yep, Joe really worked for that one," Mayor Tom continued. "I think he said he tracked that buck clear across Jenkins Mountain and back again before he ever took a shot. Buster, that's some huntin'."

The old man knew it couldn't be true, not only because they were sharing the same mountain and they never crossed tracks, but also because Styles was known for telling the tallest of tales. Most of them were recognizably flawed from the very beginning. Styles was poor at remembering the details of his creations. People, places, and events were categorically changed with each recounting. In any case, the old man heard the shots down near the beaver pond around eleven that morning and that was proof enough that Styles didn't have enough time to crisscross the mountain.

"Here ya go, sweetie," Shirley said with a big smile as she set the breakfast plate down in front of the old man. "Enjoy!"

"Thanks, Shirley."

Mayor Tom stuck his nose in front of the big plate of eats and nudged the old man.

"Hey, that sure does look good! Nothin' like sittin' down early in the morning when it's cold out and eating a hearty steak and egg breakfast with friends like I have here at Maude's!"

"Hey Shirley, I'll have the same. How's Oscar doin'? Is he ready to cook up another steak? Boy, I'll tell ya, he does some job back there. Did you know, Elmer, that old Oscar gets up at three AM every morning so he can be here to prepare and cook when the doors open at four?"

Mayor Tom gave a wave to the Mexican.

"God bless ya, Oscar!"

Oscar gave the mayor a half-smile and a lazy wave before finding the smallest and fattiest T-bone to fix for Mayor Tom's breakfast.

"!Come mierto!!**," muttered the Mexican, loud enough for only the pots and pans to hear.

Mayor Tom continued his usual banter.

"Shirley, you look especially nice this morning! I'll tell ya what, I think this job really agrees with you, 'cause you have certainly found the secret for keeping that hourglass figure. If I weren't married," Mayor Tom said with a laugh, "well, ya know!"

The old man kept to himself, so consumed with the hot plate of food that he barely noticed the Mayor's nosing up to Shirley or the reply if there was one. Oscar was timely and efficient with breakfast and before Mayor Tom could get out another word he had a plate in front of him along with the check for two eggs, a T-bone steak, refried potatoes, coffee, and toast.

"Oh well," the Mayor said under his breath with a painted on grin as he stared down at the check, "was worth a shot!"

The egg yolks ran into the steak and potatoes, but the old man didn't care. He enjoyed every bite of breakfast.

He cut up a big, juicy hunk of the red meat, sopped up as much yolk as the meat could hold, and forked it into his mouth. Next the refried potatoes were used like a sponge to sop up as much yolk as they could hold before being devoured.

From a booth directly behind him, the old man heard two hunters discussing just over a whisper what took place the day before. It sounded as though one of the hunters had shot at but missed a big deer. The old man leaned on the counter with one arm and sipped his coffee, all the while trying hard to stay still enough to hear all the words and still look unconcerned. He thought the one voice to be Frankie Cantone, which meant the other must be his half-brother Pete. Pete was the game warden. If the first was Frankie, then it was logical that the other would be Pete because they always hung together. In any case, the old man knew enough not to turn around. He didn't know them very well, only that both had been in a bad accident some time back and it showed. Both had scars about the face and lips, and one talked with a heavy lisp. The old man had heard stories of where their scars came from, as most folks in town knew, though none talked openly about the subject. Only one thing was certain, and that was someone gave them a vicious beating. They were both in their late thirties. Other than that, the only other thing about them that the old man knew was not to trust them. Some years earlier, the old man had lost a buck that he had shot and tracked only to have the trail end with entrails and guts and no buck. The old man had found out later that a Cantone boy had taken credit for being on Jenkins Mountain that very day and claimed to have shot and bagged a nice buck. But the old man remembered well that there were no other shots heard on the mountain that day. He remembered all too well that someone had dragged out a sizeable deer, his deer. The trail did not go down the mountain and through the orchard the way a proud and noble hunter would drag a deer, but instead it was dragged around through the woods just inside the wood line of the apple orchard and out the north side of the orchard to the road. Someone wanted to stay clear of other hunters and the apple farmer who lived below. In any case, the only clear fact that Elmer was absolutely sure of was that neither appeared to be very trustworthy.

The conversation from the two hunters carried on just above a whisper and sounded extremely intense, but the old man couldn't make out any other details. Then the talk went dead. "Sounds like they're in a bind," said Mayor Tom with a grimace.

"I wouldn't know," replied the old man bluntly.

Taking one last sip of coffee, the old man decided it was time to leave. He left a few dollars on the counter and grabbed his hat. "See ya, Mayor."

"Okay Elmer, good to see ya. Good huntin'! I wish I could be out there with ya, but my back is giving me problems."

Elmer was already out the door when Mayor Tom braced his back with his hands. He turned to see if anyone was listening. "I got a bad back." Looking behind him to the two in the booth, he was surprised to see the two faces looking back at him. "Hello Mayor. How's things?"

"Hello Frank. Hello Pete," answered Mayor Tom in a nervous tone. "I'm doing good. How's your aunt doing? I haven't heard from her in a couple days, so I thought she might be sick."

"No, she's doin' okay, ya know how it is."

Mayor Tom was uneasy around the Cantone boys. They were not well liked by the townsfolk. Many thought them to be crooked, which they were, and they also had for a mother and aunt a woman of callous character. She had hard eyes and a stern voice. She was sharp with words and current on all matters concerning the town. Some said she stayed sharp because she hadn't been laid since her son Pete was conceived. Mayor Tom believed this to be the case and even thought of finding a hired gun, not to shoot her, but to bag her so as she might loosen up on her public scrutiny of the job he was doing.

"Going out hunting today I see. Well, there's a lot a nice spots, I hear," said the Mayor nervously.

"Oh yeah, what do ya hear?"

Chapter 23

THEY WERE CALLED the Cantone boys, among other names, but they were not brothers. The two men were cousins and only one, Frankie, had the Cantone name. The other was Pete Aiello, but because Pete's mother's maiden name was Cantone, and she was such a dominant figure in town, a leading member of the Daughters of the American Revolution, chairperson of the Ladies Auxiliary, curator of the town library, and chief nemesis of Mayor Tom, the Cantone name is what stuck. She reverted back to her maiden name when Pete's father ran off with another woman when Pete was just a baby. He kept the Aiello name, although he rarely used it except for legal documents such as a birth certificate and driver's license. Frankie's father was killed in a queer construction accident when Frankie was five, and so the two cousins, being roughly the same age, grew up together, raised primarily by Alice Cantone, whom the town, mockingly, called Auntie Alice.

The two cousins were at best misfits. As kids they were always in trouble. They were below average students who behaved badly in the classroom. If not for the Cantone name and the vocal force of Auntie Alice behind it, the boys would have been thrown out of school before either of them reached the eighth grade. Surprisingly, they were never in trouble with the law; that is to say, they had never been to jail. The two boys were raised in the Catholic faith, although it was doubted that either of them ever prayed for anyone or anything. The two never learned the true meaning of friendship, for they never had any real friends. They had each other and they had Alice Cantone and that was all they had. But that was enough to get by in a small town. What they wanted was more, and though they had not the means to get what they wanted legally, there were bad people who could help. They knew of those types down in the city. In the city, there were bad people, and bad people could always find other bad people. The Cantone boys got connected as teenagers by doing jobs for thugs and losers. In return they got money, cars, and some occasional business down at the auto repair shop that the two high school dropouts would eventually own as partners.

The two as young men were no more well behaved than when they were in grade school; however, they did become accustomed to being friendly with the townsfolk. After all, they were small business owners who needed the town's car repair business. They often frequented the town diner and Vince's barbershop, and always with a deal for someone.

"Hey, if ya bring ya car in, we'll hook ya up with a sweet deal. Okay?"

Marty the butcher knew the Cantone boys and what they were all about. Not only was Marty a good judge of character, he also had friends in high and low places. He knew that the Cantone boys, like their fathers before them, were connected with some bookies and mob boys down in the city. Neither cousin was in too deep, but Marty kept a close watch on them. Whenever either of them entered his butcher shop, Marty always asked for cash up front. Whether it was some chops for Auntie Alice, or a job done on a deer, Marty always got the money up front. And there was never as much as a raise of an eyebrow from either of the Cantones. The request was met in full, no questions asked. Marty knew better than most that when it came to the Cantone boys, you never turned your back on them. They were crooked. Even when they came into his shop with business, even when they came with smiles on their faces and money in their hands, it was wise never to look away. Would they kill? That's the one question Marty thought of often, whenever there was mention of the Cantones. Would they kill? Possibly, but only if they could get away and get away clean. No trace. No eyes on them and not a trace of evidence to point to. A need so great as to kill a man is usually over money, and Marty never had enough to be on the wrong side of the draw. There might be someone in town, but whom, Marty couldn't figure. Theft, heist, and trespassing were more likely scenarios for the Cantones, as these crimes, although mischievous, were not deadly.

They were never caught lifting the jewelry from Peterman's Department store; never caught hotwiring a convertible out on the edge of town; never caught jacking deer at night from the road; never caught trespassing on posted property, but it all happened. It all happened, and on multiple occasions that some folks in town had some ideas as to who was behind it all. There was never any proof. No trace. No one had the goods on the Cantone boys, except for one. But the one with all the goods decided to keep it on the hush side. This one decided that matters could be handled internally. Acts of stealing, of violence, of terrorism, could be dealt with efficiently and settled without the use of peace officers and judges. The one with the goods on the Cantones had met up with them years before when they were fresh out of high school. The story was an exclusive, only to be told man to man, and it was a good one.

Chapter 24

OLD MAN JENKINS walked in the kitchen door of his seventh generation farmhouse just after six. He carried a basket half-filled with fresh eggs from the chicken coop in back of the barn. It was a cold, frost-covered morning at the farm. He went to the stove, put on a pot of coffee, and blew on his long bony fingers.

"It's a chilly one this morning," he announced to the walls.

The walls spoke back, often in the language of creaks and spiritual groans, the kind that made him feel that family never really moves on, they only become harder to see and much more tolerable on the ears. When the coffee was ready, he poured himself a hot cup and took in the aroma. While examining the contents of the basket, he heard a trucks engine growl and looked up at the kitchen window to see the lights beam against the barn and then the growl fell silent and the barn went black. A truck door slammed shut and Jenkins, with cup in hand, went out the kitchen door to see who it was that paid him a call so early in the morning.

"Hello out there!"

"Hello back, it's me, Elmer!"

"Elmer ya ol' fool, what are ya doin' out here this time uh mornin'? Don't ya know a big storm is comin'?"

The old man walked across some frosted grass and up to the stairs of the back porch.

"Oh, I thought I'd take a little walk up on the hill and see if I can get what I came for. How are ya, Abe?"

The old man extended a hand. Jenkins shook it and answered,

"Doin' okay, Elmer, and how 'bout yerself?"

"Well," the old man said, "'cept for a little arthritis, achy bones, morning gas, evening heartburn and poor eyesight, I can't complain."

Jenkins laughed, "You and me both! Hey, come on in and sit a bit, fur ya go out, and Ah'll poor ya a hot cup uh coffee."

The old man would have liked to decline on account of the time, but when the aroma hit his nose he found himself leaning his rifle against the side of the porch and walking in through the kitchen door. *Besides,* he thought, *it's difficult to say no to anything this old apple farmer asked because he had a way of pulling you in and captivating you with his many stories of life on the historic farm.*

Jenkins was a tall, wiry, weathered man standing just over six feet four with greasy, combed over white hair; long, hairy potato-slice shaped ears; and a long, leathery face that was shaved minus a day and a half. He was a tough old farmer and the head of this historic house and apple farm for the better part of half a century. He more than looked the part with his long, dry, cutup, calloused hands. Running them over his scruffy beard as he did often before going into one of his stories, the traces of hard work were even more evident in the dirt-ridden fingernails and deformed, long, bony fingers. Like many of his generation, Jenkins was schooled up to the seventh grade before dropping out to take on a more prominent role on his father's farm. From there he was home-schooled in the proper management of a four hundred acre apple farm. He learned and practiced the trade of producing a cash crop, finding a buyer for the crop, and freight contracts to get the crop to market. Just as his great, great grandfather Abraham Jenkins the first had helped in the war effort by accommodating Revolutionary War troops, so too did this Abraham by producing and selling his crop to the U.S. government in order to feed troops in World War I and again in the second World War. As other farms slowly died from lack of good economic sense, the Jenkins farm kept pushing right along, slow but steady, never a big gain, but thanks to this home-schooled farmer, never a financial loss. Even through the worst of the Great Depression, when other farms vanished overnight, the Jenkins farm managed to show a two hundred dollar profit at the fiscal year end of 1933, a feat that Jenkins was most proud of through all the years as head of the family business.

"So Elmer," said Jenkins with a smile, "what is it that ya come fer?"

The answer Jenkins had no doubt about, but the thought of asking was too much to keep held within.

"Well, I thought I'd go back on your hill and bag me the biggest buck that this town or this whole damn county has ever seen. Maybe put all those young hotshots that call themselves hunters to a long rest."

Jenkins listened with his back to the old man as he poured the hot coffee into two mugs. The steam seemed to flourish in the mugs and the aroma couldn't be beat in any fancy, faggy French coffee house. *This was man coffee*, thought the old man.

"Here ya go, Elmer. Ain't even re-cooked. Just brewed it fer you got here. Ah make it strong, but it does the job. Hey, speakin' uh them big bucks, have a seat, 'cause ah gotta story fer ya."

The two men sat at the kitchen table. Two icons of their generation, they sat, coffee in hand, and talked, for the most part, just to talk.

"Ya know," said Jenkins with interest, "Ah heard some shots yesterday up on the hill and was hopin' it was you. Ah saw yur truck on the side here and thought you'd be comin' fur it. Thought you might even come fur ma tractor and wagon too, just in case ya didn't wanta pull 'em through the orchard. Was gettin' a little curious when Ah hadn't seen ya and yur truck was still there at dark. Was sittin' down to supper when ya finally got back to yur truck and Ah thought, well, Ah guess that wasn't Elmer doin' all that shootin', cause if it was he'd probably have two or three them deer with all the shootin' goin' on."

Elmer laughed, "At least three."

"Well anyway," continued Jenkins, "Ah finished up supper and took the truck into town to see what all the hubbub was about, ya know, with all the festivities goin' on, and who Ah run into but Tom Delaney. Mayor Tom, as some might call him. Well, let me tell ya, if he ain't the shady side of a nickel then Ah don't know who is. But anyway he said that Joe Styles got a monster buck on ma property. Ah thought well okay, Ah got no problem with him huntin' on ma property. There are worse people out there than him. Wouldn't mind if he comes to see me and ask properly like a man should, ya know, to hunt and such. But fur now, that's that. Turns out Joe got that buck just on the north side uh the beaver pond and Ah thought well that makes sense 'cause that's where Ah heard all that shootin' goin' on. So anyway, Ah walked up the street to the movie house and saw Joe's buck laid out on the sidewalk. Funny thing is he probly shot up four uh ma hickory trees tryin' fur that one measly little buck!"

"Well," said the old man, "I saw that buck some weeks back. My Brittany kicked 'em out of some brush when we was bird huntin', and again I saw the deer yesterday, about ten hours too late, unfortunately. But I have to tell ya, that was as big a deer as I've seen on this mountain in quite a long time!"

Jenkins just laughed as he sipped from his mug, "Not me, not me!"

The old man, although curious, sat patiently as the apple farmer sipped his coffee and mused with pride at his secret. When he was ready, he began.

"This mountain may be small enough to hunt bottom to top in one day if you're walkin' hard, and still don't mind comin' out uh the woods an hour after dark, but it's also big enough to hide the best kept secrets. Ah must say uh the seventy five years A've been workin' this farm, A've just about seen ever livin' creature on four legs and two wings. Everything from black bear to timberwolf to mountain lion A've seen on this here mountain. In fact, Ah remember when Ah was just a kid, Ah had a pup that Ah named … ah … Ah can't remember the name, but anyhow, ma Pa wanted that pup on a rope to stake out in the apple field on the north side to keep the deer out, ya know. Anyway, that pup was runnin' with me one day while Ah was bailin' out a top field and a bobcat came rippin' outa the woods just before dark and stole that pup. Ah can still see it like it was yesterday's apple crumb pie, comin' outa them trees and grabbin' that pup in its jowls and runnin' back in the woods. Pa and Ah hunted that bobcat the very next mornin' but never saw hide or hair uh him, 'cept fur some cat prints left behind and that pup's collar, but that was about it. Saw lots uh stuff as a kid, even some old axe handles and some nails from when the troops were here fur that one winter; 'course the museum people have most uh that stuff by now. Have to really look hard to find any uh those remnants 'round here anymore. That stuff's a part uh our history and so the museum folks have turned over just about every stone lookin' fur stuff. Ah still find a horseshoe or arrowhead from time to time, and that's always fun."

Elmer sat in silence, empty coffee mug in hand, enamored by the tales of the apple farmer. Jenkins was calm and monotone in his narration of a story, but always with wonder in his eyes and at times a grin or even a smile on his face.

"But anyhow," continued Jenkins, "Ah'd have to say that the most impressive sight Ah've seen round here was just four nights ago when we had one uh them what'd ya call … lunar eclipses. And so 'bout eight, maybe eight thirty Ah went out and walked up the hill here so Ah could get a good look at it, and ya know it was a cold, crisp night, and clear as a bell, not a cloud in the sky, and ya know all the stars was out that night, and the moon was nice and full but it looked purple sittin' up there high in the sky, nice 'n plump."

"'Bout halfway up the hill, Ah heard him snort. Ah knew it was him cause Ah could smell the musky scent of a deer against the cold air. Smells so bad it made ma eyes water, and ya know that's when Ah knew it must be a big one. And let me tell ya, only a big buck can snort the way this guy snorted. Ah have to tell ya it scared the shit out uh me 'cause it sounded like a truck engine startin' up cold and cuttin' clear cross the night. Ah didn't expect it, caught me off guard. Ah mean this snort echoed through the valley and Ah swear it shook any uh the leaves still left on ma apple trees. That's when ya know there's a big deer out there!! And like Ah said, it was as clear a night as we've seen 'round here in quite a long time, and that moon was sendin' a nice right glow down upon ma orchard. Kinda felt like God was puttin' me and ma orchard on center stage, at least until Ah heard that big beast snort. Ah tell ya, that's when Ah knew that the center stage belonged to him and not me and ma orchard. Further ahead uh me, up on the hill, in between two rows uh apple trees, standin' with a doe to either side, stood the biggest buck Ah've ever seen in ma life, and Ah mean standin' right in front uh me or painted on a Christmas card. This guy was bigger than ma imagination, and ya know folks say Ah gotta big one," Jenkins joked with a raised brow.

The old man was mesmerized by the apple farmer's story, but felt an unquenchable need for more information about this beast, this king of the woods, information that Jenkins could not supply fast enough or in language that was definitive. It left the old man reeling. He wanted to pull on Abraham's shirt collar and shake him hard and demand that the story was not exaggerated or false. He wanted to know more. Jenkins continued.

"At first Ah thought the trees must be obstructin' ma view and that Ah was mistaken the branches fur this deer's rack. Anyway, Ah just stood quiet and still and squinted. Puzzled, Ah thought them darn tree branches was playin' awful bad tricks with ma eyes, makin' 'em work harder in the evenin' light. So anyway Ah looked real careful and Ah traced every part that massive silhouette, thinkin' maybe the body was really two deer, one standin' right behind the other and just a little off to one side. But ya know Elmer, that wasn't comin' together fur me, so Ah followed every part uh this outline from the hoofs right on up its skinny legs to this hefty chest and then the shoulders. Ah have to tell ya Elmer that once Ah got to the chest uh this guy Ah was startin' ta think that the branches was tellin' the truth. This guy had one fat neck and let me tell ya, he needs every bit of it! The rack," Jenkins stood up and extended his arms up to the heavens, the excitement too much for him to contain, "the rack was just massive!"

The old man stood up, a chill ran down his spine, and the palms of his hands ran sweaty and porous.

"Ya don't say!" exclaimed the old man with a wide-eyed sense of wonder and appreciation.

Still standing and holding his arms out above him, Jenkins continued.

"There in the middle uh ma field under the bright light uh the moon stood a king with his harem and me. Ah felt miniscule compared to this beast standing up on the hill, and he let me know it. He stared at me like he owned the whole mountain, bought and paid fur. He

148

musta been thinkin', *What is this smelly thing doin' on ma property, while ah'm tryin' ta make it with these nice young ladies?*"

Jenkins' arms fell back down to his sides and the two men stared at each other, the one in disbelief at what he had just heard, and the other in utter amazement at what he had witnessed but had been unable to come to grips with. Jenkins held his right hand in the air with his palm facing the old man, and like a politician getting sworn into elected office he offered his oath.

"Elmer, Ah swear that what Ah tell ya is the truth. This buck stood in ma field as the King uh Jenkins Mountain, and Ah say king not because Ah think he is, but because he thinks he is! Ah have never seen any creature as magnificent as this buck and Ah doubt Ah ever will again. Ah walked up through the orchard once since then, round the same time uh evenin', but Ah didn't see him. A buck like that, ya probly only see once if yur lucky at all. If it wern't fur the fact that deer and apple farmers don't exactly live in harmony, Ah'd say Ah was proud to have 'em on ma property. Ah, shit, Ah'm proud ta have 'em anyway!"

Elmer took a seat and thought for a moment.

"I saw some tracks a few weeks back while I was bird hunting, and I suppose they could have been from the same deer. I may have mistaken them for the buck that Joe Styles shot. Come to think of it, those tracks were bigger than Joe's buck. After hearing your story, I'd be willing to bet that the tracks along with the mutilated tree that Bo and I saw were probably from your king."

Jenkins shrugged his shoulders and took a sip of coffee.

"Well anyway," continued the old man, "thanks for the great story, Abe. Sounds interesting."

As Elmer pulled some gloves from his coat pockets, Jenkins gave the old man some advice.

"Elmer, there's one thing ya got to know! This deer's a night owl. A buck like this is smart to come out at night. They call 'em night bucks 'cause they come out and move around only after it gets dark, and they're about as hard to find during the day as a flea on a football field! Ah've known men to hunt this mountain and run themselves silly on sign and never come close to seein' what it is they're huntin' fur. They run themselves ragged and all fur nothin'! So I'm just warnin' ya to be careful so as it don't happen to ya!"

"Well Abe, I kinda feel like I'm on borrowed time anyway, so running ragged up and down your mountain chasing this guy is something that a lotta folks wouldn't mind doing and neither would I. Think I'd like to get a glimpse at just one buck like the one you just described before I die, and I bet you any real hunter would."

"Well," chimed in Abraham with a grin, "you just mentioned two key points. The first is gettin' just a glimpse, and the second is seein' 'em before ya die, and Ah guess that means seein' just a glimpse rather than him passin' ya by after you've dropped dead on one uh his runnin' paths!!"

The picture the old man imagined was of just that, and he couldn't help but laugh.

"Just think of me all spread out along the trail near one of his grand scrapes and him standing over me with his hooves bouncing up and down on my chest! Jesus, wouldn't that be a sight? Thanks again for the story," said the old man as he put out a hand, "I better get after him before the day ends."

The two walked out the kitchen door onto the porch. Jenkins sniffed the morning air.

"There's a storm comin'. It's gonna be big. Ah can feel it in ma bones. Ah bet the deer will be on the move all day if that's the case, the first one uh the season always has 'em on the move. He might just be out and about this mornin'. Well, good luck to ya Elmer!"

The old man walked down the steps of the porch with his rifle cradled under his arm. At the bottom step he stopped. He had known Abe all his life, and knew that he was a good-hearted person who did what was right, but that loneliness just had a way with some people. Abe loved to talk and there were many people available to listen. The old man knew this all too well. Some information was more valuable than others, depending on who was listening. Certain folks could take advantage.

"Hey, Abe, that story you just told me about the buck … well, you wouldn't have happened to mention it to anyone, ya know when you went into town last evening? I mean you wouldn't have said anything to Mayor Tom or anyone like that? Would you?"

Jenkins had not mentioned the big buck he saw when he went into town that night. He talked to a number of folks he knew, folks that he hadn't seen in ages, and there was so much catch up speak that an in-depth conversation about a deer in his field never came up. He saw Marty the butcher, and Ed Sprague from Sprague's Hardware, and yes, he did run into Mayor Tom, who informed him of the buck Joe Styles shot, but no conversation of the big buck ever came from it. Jenkins rubbed the top of his head and thought a moment.

"Ya know Elmer, Ah don't believe it never came up."

The old man grinned and turned to walk away.

"Hey Elmer," Abraham said in a sincere and brutally frank tone, "in the end it really don't matter. We're men uh providence, you and Ah, the last uh the old timers. Ya just keep yur eye on the prize. Don't take yur eyes off the prize. Ah mean the big picture. The one ya ain't spoken uh yet."

The old man was confused as to what Jenkins was referring to, but listened carefully to the ghostly tone in his voice.

"There's somethin' 'bout this mountain and this land. Ah tell ya, there's somethin' up there that's special. Ah been say'n it fur years; it provides fur those who are true to it. Just got to be true, that's all."

The ghostly tone together with Jenkins intense stare sent chills down Elmer's back. "I'll be seeing ya, Abe."

Jenkins grinned, "So long, Elmer."

Chapter 25

A**FLOCK OF GEESE** flew out of the northern sky. They kept on with purpose, high in the sky just visible above some low-moving clouds. A "V" of about one hundred in all honked across Jenkins' fields. The old man watched them cut across the violet sky, black jets of the great northern stratosphere, flying to complete their mission. Ol' Gray stood quiet and peaceful in the warmer confines of the barn. Upon hearing the traffic high in the sky and the footsteps in the mud out near the corral, the plow horse decided to join the visitors both near and far in welcoming a new day to the valley. It was an overcast morning, a little grayer than usual, with a drab, almost deaf feel to it. Other than the geese, the horse, and the old man, nothing had a sound to it. The land laid perfectly still, the epitome of the calm before the storm.

"Good morning, Ol' Gray. You're out awful early this morning. Did those geese wake you?"

The old man took an apple from his hunting coat, as was his custom, and hand fed it to the appreciative tail-waving old horse.

"Your friend Bo isn't with me today. No, he's stayin' home today. I better load up."

Taking four cartridges from his belt, he fed them into

the chamber and forced the lever shut. As the plow horse watched, the old man took aim at a shriveled leaf on an apple tree some fifty yards away.

"Boom!" he whispered.

He brought the rifle down to his side and then up again, this time faster, testing his skill of lifting, aiming, and shooting.

"Boom!"

The horse watched him do this again, "boom," and again, "boom," and again, "boom," each time faster than before. Satisfied with the way the rifle rested against his shoulder and the speed with which he could pick up and zero in on a target, he took the gun sling strap in his hand and slung the rifle over his shoulder. He gave Ol' Gray a pat with a glove between the eyes,

"Well my friend, let's see what the mountain has in store for us today!"

The plow horse let out a low, guttural whinny and waved his tail back and forth as he watched the old man walk the dirt road up the hill that separated the north and south orchards. He got smaller and smaller and Ol' Gray watched him until he was out of sight.

By the time the old man got to the top of the orchard, morning was just beginning to awaken the Western world and the sky changed from violet to a pale blue. The frost-covered grass twinkled ever so slightly as day began its weak approach. Millions upon millions of tiny crystals appeared out of the darkness and all paid good morning from the valley below. The old man took a brief respite and settled his eyes down on the valley so deep. Hundreds upon hundreds of apple trees rested still as if they weren't really there, but painted upon the landscape in drab colors, except for the very distant ones where the first rays of day crept over the top of Jenkins Mountain. And then it hit him, the aroma of burning hickory, whisked up the hill by a gentle breeze, the musk fragrance of autumn. It came back to him again, those days when life was young and spry. The salty, smoky smell of hickory in the cool morning air brought back the simplicity of life in the small town, the way it once was but could never be again. Looking back, the struggles to raise a family, to pay the mortgage, and clothe and feed the kids, pay for their schooling, and still have money to spend on Christmas gifts and birthdays—it wasn't so hard. It was just something you did and you sweated over it with pride, and you knew that your neighbor was in the same boat you were in, dealing with the same strains, twists, and turns of life. At the end of a hard day, the family sat at the kitchen table and with a cooking fire burning away in the stove and prayed for the bounty before them, and later the little ones were tucked into bed with wishes of sweet dreams and the promise of another day. The smoke from Jenkins' chimney brought it all back again and again. It brought back the farmer in the field with his sons chopping and stacking the wood. And the many walks with father and brothers could not be forgotten, up the great hill of Jenkins' orchards to the foot of the mountain. The wood and the salty smell it makes when it burns, along with the apple farm, might just be the only things that haven't changed over the last one hundred years. The old man pondered this as he faced the valley below with a quiet, reflective gratitude. It was a nice thought. To see one's family once again through a land unchanged by time and undisturbed by its neighbors; to remember the little things and realize that they really meant so much, that they meant everything because it was a part of who you were and why you came back to it again and again. The old man understood it, just like Abraham Jenkins understood it. These were men of character who, in an era of change, still looked to the simple things and a way of life that was all their own, not meant for everyone or to be shared with just anyone. The valley below was viewed through the eyes of a seventy-four-year-old man longing to make his way home again. It was time to go. He took a deep breath, turned, and disappeared into the woods.

Chapter 26

VINCE'S BARBERSHOP WAS open on Saturdays from 7:00 AM to 1:00 PM. No boys under the age of fourteen allowed in on Saturdays. A haircut and a shave are two dollars, but the stories and loose talk are free. Saturdays were busy days for the Sicilian barber and entertaining as well. One barber, one chair, but who cares; it's Saturday and men got time to whittle the current events while someone else sits in the chair and risks their ears against Vince's scissors.

Vince's Barbershop was the place for casual talk. It was the one true sanctuary left in life where the modern day man, looking to get away from wife, girlfriend, and even his own mind, could go and tell his side of the story, or at least hear the other side of any story. In this place of respite there was only one side to any story and that was the one you wanted to believe. On Saturday mornings, democracy started here. And it was respected. Sure, heated debate among the patrons broke out all the time. "Truman did a good job. Hey, he ended the war."

"Yeah, yeah, he still isn't as good as FDR, and ya know Truman should have used the bomb in Korea to teach those slant-eyed gook commies a lesson."

"Well now, we got the General; good republican when he's not playin' golf."

"What about spring training? Only four months away. The Yankees in '55 should have a hell of a team. Mantle will never be as good a center fielder as DiMaggio, and I don't care what nobody says."

"Leave my ears alone with that nonsense."

"Hey, what about Mays, the 'Say Hey Kid.' What about that?"

Vince's Barbershop had limitations without limits, broad spectrum ideas filtered through the minds of shallow men. Thoughts popped up like crocuses in springtime, words spoken without thought were like tulips in full bloom after a spring rain shower. They just came out.

But only days before the start of deer season, the place where casual conversation mixed with politics, humor, wit, and endless storytelling grew unusually quiet. The usual patrons, the ones who had as much need for a haircut as a cat has a need for socks, were nowhere in sight. They were off readying themselves for the hunt. Excavating a hunting spot, someplace in the woods or on a mountain, or on the corner of a cornfield or apple orchard that would make for a fine spot to see a buck come through.

No one knew the location of a good hunting spot, but the whole world had ears. Even the walls had ears, and some even decided that thinking too much in public places sent signals that could be used by others. A lead as to the whereabouts of a big buck was hard to find.

It was on the Saturday before the great hunt that Mayor Tom walked into Vince's Barbershop to find

Abraham Jenkins sitting in the chair holding court with seven other younger citizens of the town. Vince's scissors were in mid-pause just above Abe's right ear as he spoke. Not only was this the place for the casual speak, but it was also here that the local history of the town was refined and recanted for posterity. And who better to tell it than an old apple farmer. Abraham had a gift for storytelling, and here in this saloon of speak and Barbisol, the apple farmer was considered the hall of famer come home. The place fell silent to his words. Abraham had told the story a thousand times over and yet their always seemed to be a new face, a younger face who wanted to hear the story, or at least to hear it again straight from the man. Abraham loved to tell the history of his farm, the farm of his father and grandfather and great grandfather, the land of his youth, his heritage, and his patriotism.

The story always started the same ….

"Ma great-grandpapa, five generations removed from yours truly, Abraham Benjamin Jenkins settled on the land just outside uh town in the year uh our lord 1765. He was twenty years uh age and had just finished his tour uh duty in the colonial militia servin' under the British up near Fort Edward. He bought a small boat and sailed down the Hudson. He fought Indians and French marauders along the way. When his vessel could make it no further, he disbanded it by fire and climbed the mountain that would eventually bear his name and to the other side he come, and down into this valley he laid his roots. Where his origins was planted or what his parents were, we have no record, and so it's uh no importance to this here story. Anyhow, he bought and paid fur the property; the records are still to this day with the town, and Ah have with ma own eyes seen the signature uh ma root, the anchor uh ma life, amen. Grandpapa believed in hard work, and so he tended to the land and built a farm. He believed in freedom and the fairness uh men. He just hated the idea that a corrupt government so far away could poke and prod folks and take away the belongin's that they fought and sweated fur—and fur ya young folks who may not fully know what Ah'm talkin' about, you may want to look up in your history books taxation without representation. The unfair taxes made his blood boil, and his loyalty fell to the little people who, standin' together, eventually beat the ever lovin' snot out uh them red coats and sent their tea lovin' butts back across the Atlantic! He could not fight in the revolution on account he had lost his hearin' from too much cannon fire in the previous war, and so he fought the fight in other ways. He and ma great-grandma clothed the troops and fed them and even sheltered them through some rough winter months.

Their ships had traveled up the Hudson and were gearin' to converge with infantry troops movin' south from Albany. On the east side of a great mountain they would meet and await further orders. While dockin' at a point on the river, they heard from some native settlers uh the hard apple cider that a fella by the name uh Jenkins had been brewin' on the other side uh the mountain, and other supplies that could be gotten there. And so they took the half-day journey over the mountain to his farmhouse. It bein' October and the winter season closin' in fast, orders were sent fur the troops to hold their position on the Hudson, set up winter camp, and await the infantry advancin' south from Albany. The troops set up camp on Abraham Jenkins' apple farm fur the entire winter uh 1777. They stayed until the middle uh March, when a surprise visit by none other than General Washington himself ordered the camp to pick up and move out. The general was not happy with the condition uh the outfit, though thoroughly bewildered by the fact that not one man had deserted durin' the rough winter months, this compliments to the well-seasoned brew that Jenkins had in his root cellar.

Nonetheless, the general expressed his displeasure at the site uh the compound, which fur whatever reason was not to his likin'. It may have been because there wasn't an adequate roadway goin' over the mountain to the ship on the Hudson. Instead, the troops had relied on a rough cart trail, often called Jenkins' Pass fur the man who made it. The trail meandered like a river from the north side to the south side, slowly gradin' its way up the mountain from the west over and down the other side to the east. The mountain was a vigorous one that had several high and steep stone ledges that made it impossible to pass straight over the top with horse and wagon. One man on foot could with a lotta care climb up through the jagged ledges usin' the rock outcroppin's to pull himself up to the next ledge. Once on top there would be some two hundred yards uh walkin' to get to the next ledge and then again with a lotta care he would have to climb some sixty feet to the next level. Fur this reason, Jenkins' Pass was used. It was a hard task let me tellya tryin' to get supplies back and forth, not to mention defense uh the ship, and fur this reason the generals' bein' more than a little peeved Ah would say was more than a little justified.

As the story goes, young Abraham Jenkins, ma

great-grandpapa was in the north field uh his apple farm repairin' a horse wagon that had lost a wheel the previous November, and so missed the sight ah what took place fur much uh that early March mornin'. Some hired hands later informed him uh the events uh that day, which the biggest bein none other than Washington himself ridin' down the middle uh ma family's orchard on a massive and majestic white horse that glowed against the backdrop uh mud and snow."

The barbershop had become intensely quiet. The teenagers and old gents alike had fallen victim to Jenkins' gift of storytelling. Even Vince's clippers were still. Vince heard the story many times. It didn't matter. All listened intently with fallen chins at Jenkins' every word. Jenkins continued.

"Accompanied by five other officers, they emerged from the woods. Once in the open field, they rode side by side with the general in the middle. They picked up the wagon trail that cut the two orchards in half, the same cart path that runs up the center uh ma property today, and that's how the general and his men first made their appearance on ma great-grandpapa's land.

It was early mornin' by the time the general and his officers reached the wagon trail in the open field. To both sides uh the muddy trail were apple trees, and some four hundred yards down the trail that turned slightly here and there was Grandpapa Jenkins' farmhouse. It was a wet, chilly mornin' and the general was feelin' a bit under the weather. Cold and aggravated, the general proceeded down the trail. If the scent uh hickory smoke in the air was not testament enough to a warm house, the smoke risin' out uh Jenkins' chimney was, and the men rode a half-hoof quicker down the hill. Washington himself commented on how he had to warm his hands and feet, fur the great hill that was Jenkins Mountain was uncompromisin' and much colder than the open fields below.

The soldiers had built wooden huts fur shelter from the frigid months. Ash was used fur buildin', as it was less knotty fur cuttin' and easier hammerin' spikes through; hickory fur campfire wood, as it burned hotter and fur longer hours at a time. There was an abundance uh both on the north end uh Jenkins' spread. On this end was a nice level piece uh property where the great hill descended into a flat that was part meadow and woods. To the east the flat extended and then dipped down into the rocky jagged northeastern slope uh Jenkins Mountain and ran straight through to the Hudson. On the western side the flat meandered and sloped slightly until it ran into the northern most corner uh Jenkins' farm. To the north uh the flat lay the hills leadin' to the first uh many ledges that made up the mountain, and to the south lay a beaver pond. In all, the flat extended about two square miles.

The soldiers had worked expeditiously from the last week in October into early November, choppin' down trees in the flat and cartin' the logs down into the apple orchard to be used in hut buildin's that could shelter on average twenty soldiers each. Many huts were needed, and the land was generous to their needs, as was Jenkins. Bein' an apple farmer he was happy to be uh service wherever he could, and not only showed them where they could harvest the best trees, but also informed them uh the many beaver that could be trapped and used fur everythin' from socks to soup, and also the big deer that lived in the swamp behind the beaver pond. With his help, the huts were completed by the second week in November, and there was plenty uh venison, turkey, beaver soup, apple pie, and hard apple cider fur the fall feast that followed.

As the officers on horseback rode down the muddy trail that separated the two fields, the general looked on at his troops. Many were huddled around campfires, some warmin' their hands, others dryin' garments uh clothin'. There was no official word uh Washington's arrival, and the sentries on duty were corralled by the generals' officers and ordered to defer their reports uh anyone comin' down the trail. And so the men went about their business, although some looked on in amazement to see this great man on a big horse that was truly magnificent, each muscle uh the beast flexin' and extendin' with such grace but with a promise uh tenacious power if needed. The men began to talk and point at the sight comin' down the trail until someone yelled out, "It's General Washington, it's the general."

The men on horseback kept ridin' as the trail began to level off. Once at the base uh the hill, the horses trotted a bit quicker, kickin' up mud as they rode, and did not stop until they reached the farmhouse. A field commander approached the officers and offered them a proper salute as well as the full service uh the New York detachment. The general scowled and gave the field officer a sharp but quick criticism fur choosin' such dreadful location fur quarters, so far away from proper defense uh the ship that lay bedded on the Hudson, not to mention lookout fur British forces that would most surely use the Hudson as their guide fur travelin' north or south. The general would not hear any defense by the officer fur choosin' such a location and with curtness as sharp as any the officers had ever heard, he gave the embarrassed field officer orders fur the outfit to be ready to march within the hour.

Conversation over, the general dismounted from his horse and the others quickly followed. He walked to the farmhouse with the officers some distance behind him and then up the steps uh the porch just off the kitchen and banged on the door. There was no answer. The general took off his gloves and with his fist in a knot pounded on the door, but there was no answer. Not wantin' to be rude or disrespectful to the owner uh the property whose hospitality was considerable, the general waited on the porch fur a moment, blew on his frozen hands, gazed out at the massive fields surroundin' the house and thought. After a moment uh reflection, the general turned and walked through the door and into the house. The officers followed the general inside and closed the door.

There in ma Grandpapa's kitchen on an early March mornin' uh 1777, stood five officers and the commander uh the Continental Army. The stove had been cranked up with wood earlier that mornin' just before Jenkins left fur work in the north field, and coffee was in a pot on top uh the stove. The general pulled up a chair next to the stove, threw his gloves on the kitchen table, and proceeded to take off his boots so as to warm his feet and hands. One uh the officers found some mugs, and the six men huddled around the stove, drank hot coffee, and warmed themselves.

What a sight ma Grandpapa Jenkins might have borne witness to had he walked in from workin' the field on that cold mid-mornin' in March. Thank God for the hired hands that bared witness to what went on in the kitchen that mornin' and so Ah'm able to pass the details along for posterity. After gettin' warm, Washington set his officers to plannin'. The bulk uh Washington's army down in Morristown, New Jersey was preparin' ta move south and the detachment presently occupying Jenkins' orchard would meet the main body in a few days at a place called Whippany, New Jersey. A map was rolled out onto the kitchen table and preparations was made. Washington's best weapon was always deception, and this may have been the main reason fur not sticken with the main body but instead ridin' north to meet this breakaway body uh the New York Brigade. In any case, plans fur troop movement was made, and the general was ready to move.

The men rolled up the map while Washington wrote a quick note with a turkey quill and black ink that an officer pulled from his knap sack that was draped over his shoulder. The note was hastily written, fur the general was anxious to ride. It read as follows:

To my good Sir Jenkins,

Whose hospitality to the Continental Army has been of good trust and most important to the cause of liberty and freedom. This I trust will find you to give my many thanks and assurance of reparations by the government of these United States.

Sincerely,
Geo Washington

The camp was packed and ready to march by late mornin', and the general with his staff started up the trail through the middle uh the two orchards. They were three-quarters uh the way up the hill, almost to the wood line, when Jenkins, who was ridin' home from the north field on the bare back of a plow horse, noticed the parade uh soldiers on the move. If not fur the huge mount that made him eye level with some young apple trees, Jenkins would have never witnessed the site at the top uh the hill. For at the head uh the parade uh marchers was a horse that was as white as an angelic figure sent from heaven, and on her back was a man uh considerable size. The horse stood still at the top uh the hill and both man and beast faced west lookin' down across the vast farm from which they came. From far away, Jenkins studied the dress uh the man; tan britches, black knee-high ridin' boots, what appeared to be a dark blue coat, and a long black cape. A saber was attached to his left hip and an officer's cocked hat topped a head uh white was a tip off that this man was uh high rank. *But this man is unique,* thought Jenkins. He rode high in the saddle like a prince or a king and yet looked to be a very good horseman.

One must be a fine horseman to ride an animal like that, Jenkins thought. *Could it be …?*

Jenkins heart raced and his mind wildly jumped to the name uh Washington, but he would not dare say the name aloud. Instead with lips clinched he squinted and pulled in the reigns uh the horse to be as still as could be. He had to get another look.

"Could it be … could it be?" Jenkins thought out loud. "My god, it is," the farmer's chin dropped to his chest. "That's *General Washinton!*"

With that, the gallant rider on the hill pulled on the reigns and the head uh the powerful beast turned one hundred and eighty degrees and darted into the woods, tail and cape featherin' out in the breeze as they disappeared from sight. The farmer felt ashamed to have said the name aloud, as if it had jinxed his eyes from viewin' his majesty. He took off his cap and wiped the sweat from his forehead. It was time to go home.

Years later, it was debated as to whether it was really Washington who rode into camp on that cold and damp March mornin'. Some say the history is too foggy to say if he was or not. But Ah'll tell ya what, Ah know the history and ma family knows it to. As fur the note, it blew of the table onto the floor as the officers exited through the kitchen door. The floor was wet from the meltin' snow from the officer's boots, and the ink ran and ran until it was virtually unreadable. When Jenkins walked through his kitchen door, all he found was six tin mugs on the table, all empty; chairs in a semicircle around the kitchen cook stove, and puddles uh water on the wooden floor, along with the handwritten note that Jenkins picked up and made out what he could. And so that's the history uh ma farm and Ah'm more than happy to pass this history along to the young folks."

Silence fell over the barbershop. Not a chair scraped the tile floor, not a cough or sneeze interrupted the artist's self-interpreted portrait of history. Vince's scissors continued their long rest. Not a single strand of hair had fallen to the floor, but this mattered none to those who waited for their turn in the mirror. When he had finished, Jenkins sat back in his chair, folded his hands on his chest under the red smock, and crossed his legs. Waving his boot out far beyond his knee, the master left it to the silence of the room to announce that he, the master storyteller, was indeed done. Mayor Tom stood just inside the doorway and wept. Being the heart of the town, the mayor felt this act would most characterize his passion and patriotism. It was a valiant political chess move on his part.

"Abe, that was some story, and you know, I'm so proud to be an American when I hear that beautiful story."

The fake tears quickly faded away and Mayor Tom was at full throttle again, sucking up the crumbs of whatever moment he could now steal.

"Good morning everyone, and good morning to you, Vince. Got a steady hand this morning? How are you, Abe? Haven't seen you in a coon's age. I hope you'll be joining us for the Harvest Moon festivities! Vince will be there."

"We're singin' in a barbershop quartet!" Vince smiled proudly.

"Tom," answered Jenkins with a laugh, "ahm uh apple farmer, Ah don't hunt deer … legally!"

"Oh! Well, I won't say a word. You know me, Abe."

"Hey, speakin' uh deer, ye'll never guess what Ah saw in ma field last night …."

The scissors clipped away. The fingers of the Sicilian barber broke free of the ice to make neat again what was disheveled and trim what was wild. When he was done and all was in order once again, the smock lifted, the farmer paid his due, and he was replaced by another who entered the chair.

"Well boys, it's been fun seein' ya."

The door opened and closed hard again with a stiff cold breeze. Jenkins, the great storyteller and legendary apple farmer who's stories came and went so easy without thought or even recollection, had exited stage right.

"Is that the greatest story ever?" asked Mayor Tom.

All agreed simultaneously that Abe's account of history, whether completely true or not, was indeed very entertaining.

"There is one other story that I've heard a few times," said the patron now sitting in the chair, "that I believe can match that story."

The patron looked at Vince in the mirror and the barber looked back with a nod and a grin.

The story the patron now sitting in the chair referred to was not about the town and its history or a plot of land or a group of people who worked tirelessly on it. It did not represent a half-truth or have fictitious legs that ran bigger and better with each retelling. This story was about one man. For no matter how great the history of the apple farm, the history of Abraham Jenkins himself had no comparison. There was a story that was told. It was about the character of the man. It was the man. It was in the man. Well, most folks young and old knew of Abraham Jenkins the apple farmer. And they knew Abraham as the longtime citizen of the town. The name Jenkins was as well known a name to the town as Abraham Lincoln was to the American Civil War. The old apple farmer was a staple, a mountain, a statue. But there was one story that made those that heard it sit up in their chairs and take notice. And it was exclusive to Vince's Barbershop. Outside it, the story was never recited. It was never mentioned. No one ever said, "That's the guy who so and so," or "Did you know who did what to you know who." The value of the story was that of truth. The story was truth. Vince had heard the story several times over the years. The barbershop grew quiet once again. Vince put down his clippers.

Chapter 27

IT HAPPENED SEVERAL years earlier during a mid September heatwave, and shortly after the two Cantone boys had opened their mechanic shop….

Pete Cantone pulled down the garage door of the mechanic shop and locked it. It was Friday, late afternoon. He set out for home on foot. It was just over three miles to his mom's house. The Pancake Hollow Road was dusty and hot. Pete pulled his greasy white T-shirt over his head, exposing his chiseled upper body. With a hand he pushed straight back the greasy mop of thick, jet-black hair and draped the t-shirt over his head. He was wiry but strong for his five-foot, nine-inch frame. His dirty, faded blue jeans fell loose around his waist. When he got to the beginning of Jenkins' farm, he stopped and rested on a stonewall. He pulled a pack of Lucky's and some matches from his pocket. Mouthing a cigarette from the pack, he lit it and blew the smoke high into the air. The hot of the day was just beginning to turn. It would be a pleasant late summer evening. The sun was setting over the valley. Its soft amber rays touched the hilltops to the east, leaving the apple trees and Jenkins' farm basking in the last of the day's heat. The faint bark of a dog was heard off in the distance. The trees that bordered the stone wall were full with the fall oranges, reds, and yellows. Their leaves fluttered with a faint breeze. Pete finished the cigarette and threw the butt to the ground. Standing up on the wall, he looked up the hill and over the vast spread of apple trees. They went on forever up the great hill. The plump fruit hung in bunches from the trees. The juicy reds and deep violets were too much to pass up. Pete took the t-shirt from his head and dressed. Pulling the pack of Lucky's from his pocket, he mouthed another and lit up. Exhaling, he looked up and down the road but saw no one. He took another puff and jumped off the wall and into the orchard to pick the delicious fruit. The butt hung from his lip. He walked between the rows of trees. Using his t-shirt as a basket, he picked the apples as he walked from tree to tree and row to row until his shirt was fit to bust. Pete held the end of the bulging shirt up with one hand. He took one last long drag. Holding the butt in his free hand, he looked up the hill and blew. Flicking it to the ground, he started back toward the road.

"Hey you," a voice called out from far away.

It was barely audible to Pete, and he thought it might be a voice from the farmhouse that carried in the breeze and so he paid it no mind.

"Hey you," the voice sounded again, this time noticeably louder and more distinct in its tone.

Pete, a bit startled, stopped, turned, and looked up the hill from where the voice came.

"Hey you, what the hell do ya think yer doin' in ma orchard?"

Pete couldn't make him out through the trees, but he knew the voice was up there somewhere. It was Abraham Jenkins way up on the hill. He was standing on the seat of his farm tractor. The tractor had broken down on the dirt road that split the two orchards. Jenkins was working on it when he smelled tobacco smoke. Standing on the tractor seat, he made out the white shirt walking through the orchard way down below.

"Hey, you son uh bitch!"

Abraham jumped down off his tractor. He grabbed a long handled wrench and marched down the hill.

"Put down those apples! No one told ya ta pick apples here!"

Pete could see him coming down the hill. He was a tall, lumbering man of advanced years, but he moved with conviction and with a weapon in hand besides. Pete thought it best to walk slowly out toward the road, but he didn't run. It could be said of the Cantones that they didn't run from a conflict. They were cool-headed and secure in their fighting abilities.

"Hey you down there, get back here!"

Pete stopped and turned, "Fuck you, old man!"

It was clear to Pete that the man on the hill had the temperament for a confrontation, but Pete, who was usually inclined to oblige, was in no mood to fight. He continued, cool-headed, on toward the road, a dozen apples still in his t-shirt. When he got to the stone wall, he took one last look back up the hill. The old man was still after him, with a nice-sized iron wrench clinched in his fist.

"Go on back up the hill, old man. Don't waste your energy; you don't really want a piece uh me! Just go back to doin' what you're doin'."

Pete could see that the man on the hill had no

intention of taking his advice, so he climbed over the stone wall and didn't look back again.

Abraham Jenkins burned. The sweat on his sun-baked forearms sizzled.

"Get back here, you! Ah know who ya are down there. Yer one uh them Cantone boys! Well, why don't ya come back here and A'hl show ya a piece uh me, ya skinny little bastard no good son uh bitch!"

Jenkins continued on down the hill, a tight-fisted, leathery old farmer with no shirt, skin glistening red like an Indian, and ready for battle. Jenkins, despite his age, had no problems mixing it up. If anything, he could let out some frustrations with the tractor on a Cantone boy. That would be alright with him.

"Come on back, boy, and let me serve it to ya! Come on back ya chicken-chested mamma's boy! Hey, ah bet yer mamma's got bigger balls between her legs than you got! Yup, that's what ah heard 'bout the Cantone boys; Mamma got bigger balls!"

Jenkins also didn't mind throwing insults. He was good at it. If there was a prize at the county fair for name-calling and foul language, Jenkins would win every year with a bunch of fresh, home-grown insults. The distance that separated the two was great enough that no physical altercation resulted, but the verbal cues were there, heard loud and clear, and so the gauntlet had been thrown down. The Cantone boy was out of sight. Jenkins stopped on the hill. The infuriation fizzled away. He stood on the side of the hill and watched the last of the sun's rays fade deep into the west.

The last few weeks of Indian summer settled in on Jenkins' farm. These were warm, pleasant days. The sun painted the trees, showing favoritism to the oaks and maples of the valley. And they challenged the wildflowers in the meadow with their wicked bright colors and blood reds. These days were peaceful. The nights cool. It was the apple farmer's favorite time of year. A poor farmer Abraham would never be. As long as he had his land and the trees and fields of color, as long as he had a plot to work, air to breathe, and sweat to give, then he would always be wealthy.

Picking time had come. Abraham expected a grand crop. He hired three more workers for the fall harvest. One morning while working the north field, two of the migrants came upon something quite unusual.

"Better get the boss," the one said in a Jamaican tongue to the other.

One hour later, Abraham was standing with his workers in the north field pondering over the grotesque site before them. Ten apple trees had been cut down at their base with a bucksaw. They were left fallen in the field. Next to the trees lay two dead deer. Each deer had been shot several times. Their heads were sawed open and the top part of their skulls removed for the horns. Both deer had apples stuffed in their mouths. Their stomach cavities were cut open. The entrails had been removed. The empty cavities were filled with whole apples. In disgust, the apple farmer looked around and saw that the intestines of the deer were wrapped around some of the standing trees, like a garland wrapped around a Christmas tree. It was a massacre.

After some silent moments of study, Abraham ordered his men in a low, calm voice.

"Harvest the good apples from the fallen trees, and

then load the trees onto the tractor wagon. Load up the deer and all the crap hangin' in them trees. Take 'em to the top edge uh the north field and burn 'em. Get some kerosene from the barn, and dose 'em good. Ah don't want ta see a trace uh them deer or the trees when Ah get back."

Looking hard at the lead worker everyone called Joe, Abraham demanded in a sincere tone, "Is that understood?"

"You got it, man," replied Joe in his Jamaican accent.

He looked around him one last time at the mess in his field and then back at Joe. He looked at him coolly and nodded his head. Satisfied that his orders were fully understood, he left the north field and headed back to the house. Joe watched him leave. When he was out of sight, he turned to the other worker and shook his head and sighed.

"Hell will come to the man that messes with him." He stared back in the direction of the house, "Lord, have mercy."

Abraham was in the house for only a moment. When a worker saw him again, he had a shotgun in one hand and a box of shells in the other. He headed over toward a beat-up Ford pickup. The truck was parked to the side of the barn that faced the kitchen door of the house. By appearance, the truck looked inoperable. Its original color was green. To look at it now, you never would have guessed it. The frame of the truck was so rusted that most visitors to the farm thought it was just more junk strewn about the property. Hay grew up tall around the frame, adding to the façade of neglect. And this held true when the door was pulled open. Its hinges cried the loudest for attention. Abraham got in and laid the shotgun across his lap. The ignition wires were exposed and hanging, ducked together with electrical tape. A pair of needle-nose pliers was jammed into the ignition. The pliers acted in place of the key and remained in the ignition as a permanent yet creative fixture. Abraham prided himself on his ingenuity. The pliers were turned in the ignition and the truck started smooth and purred like a pussycat. The engine growled as it tried to catch the reverse gear. When it kicked in, the truck sped backward away from the barn and into the dirt driveway. It skidded to a halt and growled again as it tried to catch first gear. Dust rose up around it. When the gear kicked in, the wheels sputtered in the dirt. A plume of dust consumed the truck. The engine raced. The little beat-up truck sped out down the driveway. Its tires peeled out as the truck turned onto Pancake Hollow Road. The sun's rays glared through the dust. The tiny suspended particles sparkled in the air. A muffled engine growl could be heard way off in the distance, trying to catch third gear.

Abraham Jenkins called it justice. Most lawyers and certainly any judge worth his salt would call it something different. In a town that had two gas stations, one on each end of town, a grocerette, a fire and police station, a movie theater, a butcher shop, a hardware store, a jewelry store, and a greasy spoon, progress and modern life was no longer available at a premium, but was something that was affordable and expected. Lawlessness and vigilantism had no place to thrive, even with a world at war. But to a small-town apple farmer, progress was everything reaped to put food on the table, and justice was found when it was served face-to-face and man-to-man. And so when knuckles cracked across the face of one Cantone boy, fracturing his cheekbone and sending him horizontal to the earth, justice was served. And when a size twelve boot caught the fallen boy in the gut, breaking his wind and curling him up like a frightened caterpillar, justice was served. And when the other Cantone boy jumped in to help his cousin, the one that was seen in the apple orchard, he found justice to be even more painful and terrible than it was for his cousin. Jenkins cracked the boy in the mouth with his twelve-gauge shotgun, bloodying his lips and breaking his front teeth.

When Pete dropped to his knees, Jenkins stood over him. He broke open the shotgun and filled each barrel with a single shell that he took from his shirt pocket. For someone involved in a fight, the old apple farmer looked uncharacteristically cool. Pete paid attention. He noticed that he breathed normal. Jenkins stared at the fallen boy with shark-like eyes as he snapped the barrel of the gun closed. Pete could feel the cold eyes upon him. The eyes made him feel broken and vulnerable. If the taste of his own blood and the gritty chunks of teeth floating freely in his mouth hadn't broken him, the cold, calculating eyes did all this and more. Death, Pete thought, was surely upon him.

Before the boy had a chance to beg for mercy, Jenkins shoved the double-barrel into his mouth with such force that the boy fell onto his backside. Pete felt the cold steel to the back of his throat. He tried to gag, but the weight of the gun and the boot that was now on his chest prevented him from moving. Despite what he must have thought the day they had the confrontation in the apple orchard, this was not a man that was over the hill. Abraham Jenkins was not the run-down old apple farmer whose bones cracked and whose muscles were too weak to perform the daily rigors of life. Instead, he was a man who was stronger both mentally and physically for having lived such a long, vigorous lifestyle. It was a fatal error on the part of the boys. And they learned in the brief few seconds that were spent together that this man would go farther than most. They saw that this man had the resolve to do what many would not, and others could not.

With the barrel resting in the boy's throat, Jenkins leaned his face up close to the stock and took aim down the long barrel.

"Ain't really necessary fur me ta take aim."

His voice was calm and cool, yet almost void of common sense.

"Guess it's just uh habit Ah have when Ah'm gonna shoot somethin'."

Without as much as a single breathe to balance his heart or steady his hands, he pushed the safety off. It clicked and the Cantones shuddered at the sound. "Hah, did that frighten ya?" asked Jenkins with an evil grin. Frankie Cantone lay in a ball behind him, and Pete only four short feet from his nose.

"Boys," he said in a low voice, just audible over the boys' heavy beating hearts, "You been causin' trouble in this here town fur some time now, and today its time ta pay the bill."

If ever there was a day when dead-end boys, the kind who never made good, felt that they were overmatched with their own brand of terrorism, this surely was that day. The Cantones thought they would surely die at the hand of a madman. A madman among us, they thought, who was crazier and nastier than the most ruthless mobster, and he was living right in our own town. Not only that, but we were stupid enough to pick on him, dumb enough to steal from him, and naïve enough to vandalize his property and not think once of reprisal. Pete felt the heavy barrel ease up on his throat and he coughed on the blood. He turned his head away to cough up some of the blood and teeth, but this seemed to anger the farmer. The barrel forced his head straight again and the steel felt heavy once again on the back of his throat.

"Ya know, Ah wouldn't make any sudden movements if Ah were you. Ma hands ain't nearly as steady as they used ta be. Ya know, Ah wonder. Ah wonder if Ah were ta blow yur head into hamburger and gut shoot yur buddy over there, do ya think anybody'd give a barn full uh rat shit about it?"

Jenkins removed his hand from the trigger and cradled the gun in one arm but kept the barrel pointed down the boy's throat. Pete watched him take a pouch of plug from his pocket. His boot pressed heavier on Pete's chest. He shoveled the moist brown leaves into his mouth and chewed until he had a wad balled up in his right cheek. He rolled up the pouch, placed it back in his shirt pocket, and replaced his hand on the trigger.

"Sure, yur Mama might cry … maybe. And she might demand reparations, but that'd be it. No one in town or clear cross this county would care 'cause they'd already knowed you boys are up ta no good, and they'd think ya messed up with some uh them boys down in the city ya been hangin' out with. They'd investigate and satisfy themselves that was the case and that'd be the end of it. No one would care, no one. And things around these parts would get back ta normal in a few weeks at the longest. The town would be grateful ta whoever it was that done it. 'Course, they wouldn't say so cause it wouldn't be proper, but they'd be thinkin' it. And ya know why? Cause you two are fleabag, dead-end boys that can't be saved. You're two uh the worst kind uh seeds that grew, but ah tell ya somethin', one thing Ah can do is sure keep ya from gettin' old, Ah tell ya that much."

The boys lay frozen. Neither one moved a muscle or breathed a distinguishable breath. They took in every word. It may have been the first time in all their lives that either of them really listened so completely. Jenkins took the barrel of the gun out of Pete's mouth and walked over to Frankie, who was still doubled up like a caterpillar. He spit a mouthful of juice onto the grass just beside Frankie and wiped his chin of the excess.

"Well boy, what do ya think?"

With his boot to Frankie's shoulder, he pushed the boy onto his back. He shoved the barrel of the gun into his belly.

"What'd you have fur breakfast, boy? I know it wasn't venison sausage, 'cause that's still layin' in ma field!"

Jenkins shoved the gun in deeper into his gut so that the end of the barrel was consumed by the boy's stomach. Frankie moaned.

"You want me ta open ya up right here and now?"

Frankie closed his eyes. It was too much for him to take. His body went limp. He resigned himself to a bloody fate. Totally helpless in his departure, his nerves had given up and fear no longer served a purpose in his body. His breathing grew faint and the earth felt as if it was slipping down around him. His body felt heavy, but his soul was light. It drifted off away from his body. It was gray, the place that his soul went to, and it was lonely. Where he was he hadn't a clue. The surroundings were familiar yet it was not a place he knew well. He was standing on a rock on the edge of a swamp. The swamp ranged in all directions. The water looked deep but still. Big trees stood tall in the water, their branches, like long, bony fingers, swept outward. Hanging moss hung from the branches like vines right on down to the water. There were no leaves on the trees. The swamp was hazy and without color. He thought this place peaceful in a way in that there wasn't a man sticking a gun in his gut. The man had gone. But something was wrong. He looked around for Pete, but he was not there. Through the haze, and beyond the mossy branches, an eye was watching him. He could feel its presence. The loneliness left him, but the eye watching him was much worse. It hid among a thick cloud of gray. It had no defined shape, only a presence. The peaceful feeling about this place no longer existed. Frankie wanted out. He tried to run, but his legs would not function. He kept falling down, tripping over himself. The rock was slippery. Frankie tried to get up, but his arms were too heavy to lift his body. They were trapped under him. He was sliding off the rock. The water was too close. His eyelids felt gritty, like there was wet sand pasting his eyelashes together. They wouldn't open. They stretched as if made of rubber but would not open. Frankie tried to breathe, but the haze seemed to engulf the air, making it too thick for his lungs to consume. Fighting against the haze with clumsy shifts of his torso was all he could muster, for his arms and legs as if tied and set in concrete no longer worked.

"Uuuggh," he gasped for air and his eyelids opened.

Color returned. His eyes were open wide and staring straight up at a soft blue sky filled with thick cumulus clouds. His arms worked again, and so he sat up and looked around, still disoriented. Pete was sitting on the steps of his mom's house, spitting out what remained of his front teeth. He had blood all down his nose and chin, and his white undershirt was stained a dark red. Pete said in a weak, blood gurgling lisp, "You passed out. When he poked you with the gun, I guess you fainted."

He had trouble breathing out his mouth, and he held his hand up to his chin in obvious pain.

"He's gone now."

Chapter 28

THE OLD MAN walked the western face of Jenkins Mountain. The clouds were building up across the valley, diluting the sun's rays. The temperature slowly dropped. It was eight o'clock by the time he made it to the top of the first ledge. Sweat ran cold under his long johns. He stopped to rest on the stump of a half-rotted elm.

The king had run wild throughout the night, courting the way kings do, with a supreme, totalitarian command over his female subjects. No less the player than an Arabian sultan at an all-night orgy, the king set out to impress and complete this circle of life by impregnating the does of Jenkins Mountain. This he did again and again that by sunup, he was running a bit behind schedule getting back to the secluded safe zone deep in the heart of the mountain. This was the dangerous move that many an intruder would be waiting for, the fatal mistake that could turn a magnificent creature from hot-blooded, beastly enthusiasm into a stuffed trophy to be hung for eternity on a hunter's wall. He had not eaten in nearly four days nor lapped his swollen tongue at the water running from the brook. Not a single drop of rain pacified his pasty tongue or rinsed his frothy lips. Not even a mid-afternoon nap in the heart of the dense forest where the cool, crisp autumn air could soothe his temper was afforded him. And now with the break of day behind him, he ran at a feverish pace to make it to the high ledges of the mountain to the confines of the deep enclave of the forest.

The Cantones had gotten an early start, thanks to the gossip from Mayor Tom about a massive buck on Jenkins Mountain. They beat the old man to the woods more than a half hour before sunup. They planned on being far up into the hill and far away from the open fields of Jenkins' orchard and from the apple farmer himself. Their wounds had years to heal, but the scars and lisp speech were constant reminders of a traumatic past. But however sharp the constant reminder was, the thrill of being bad and the stupidity of it all still loomed large. The testosterone ran ugly in them as they challenged fate and set out to exhaust some measure of revenge by stealing a big buck from Jenkins' property.

Frankie Cantone cut through the southern corner of Jenkins' apple orchard under the cover of darkness and walked the swamp right through to the beaver pond. Pete cut off from his cousin at the corner of the orchard and entered the woods just north of the pond. He continued on until he was on top of the second ledge. Here he made his post. He took a smoke from his pocket and leaning on a cedar overlooking the swamp, lit up and exhaled to the heavens. With one hunter high, the other low, they expected their chances were pretty good that one of them might get a look at a big buck. It could prove to be a smart plan, as big bucks were known to hide out the day in the swamplands. The failsafe was to catch one further up on the hill while enroute to cover either high in the mountain or low in the swamp.

Chapter 29

BY NINE THAT morning the first snowflakes came, followed by more pronounced heavy gales of snow. A Canadian cold front was pushing hard through the region from the north and a warm front moved in from the west. The two fronts converged, and when they did a Nor'easter is what they created. The temperature dropped ten degrees an hour and the countryside grew restless.

The first shot had grazed the king's white underbelly. The hot (brass) missile with the jagged butt end shaved off rather close to the buck's midsection several tufts of white hair. It was the perfect shave, as not a vessel or capillary of skin was broken or disturbed. The hair fell to the earth and camouflaged quickly by the freshly fallen snow. The king had felt the bullet simultaneously as he heard the deafening roar of the gun and instantly turned his trot into an all-out run with graceful, lunging leaps and darting misdirections in between trees and uneven terrain. In a flash of a white flag, he had slipped by the uninvited hunter and was gone. The roars continued one after another, but they were no longer a threat. The cold front had blessed the king with a renewed energy, and this he wisely used to maintain his lengthy strides, running west down the mountain and then sweeping around and doubling back up the hill toward the height of the mountain. Any hunter on the king's trail would empty his tank and bag nothing but cramps and wind before his day would end in a disappointed and mysterious way. The Cantones reunited and walked the trail together until they picked up the tracks heading straight down the mountain.

"He's headin' for the blowdown down low. Let's not chase him too quick. We'll let him settle in and get comfortable. Keep your eye on them tracks though, 'cause this storm will fill 'em in quick. He's a big one though, and those tracks are mighty deep."

The old man heard the shots, as did the apple farmer down below. The erratic muffled sounds were not that of a seasoned hunter. The old man decided rather quickly that the shots must have missed their intended target and that if indeed the creator of the ruckus had shot at a deer, then the deer would not run straight away from danger, but would turn either up the mountain or down it completely or even back into it. Chased bucks are known to do a 360 degree turn, fooling the majority of amateur hunters into giving chase for miles when they would have had better luck giving chase for a hundred yards and then tracking in a giant loop back near the original start point. The old man studied the falling snow and the slight angle of the flakes as the breeze pushed them diagonally into the mountain. Just shy of a minute after the last blast was heard, the instincts of a wily old hunter kicked in and he was on the march up the next ledge of the mountain like the bounding buck. Long, purposeful strides made deep footprints in the fresh, white powder and they angled straight and true up the unforgiving mountain. The strides were not that of an old man, but of a hunter whose exoskeleton had found purpose and whose heart and lungs had found youth. Over the rocks and boulders, over the downed trees and rotted stumps, over the half-frozen mountain stream, and through the thick furs and spruce the hunter climbed with a salty, sweaty determination that ran cold on his brow as the snowflakes melted about his face and neck. The sinking temperatures ran cold in his lungs as they got sucked deeper and longer with every stride. A liberated heart pounded furiously, like pistons of an engine, trying to break out from beneath the red hunting coat; as if this organ no longer needed to work with the others of the human body, but could complete its mission independently of lungs or limbs. The ever passionate heart pounded, and funneled its exhaust through the many layers of clothing in the form of a soaking, hot perspiration. And still he continued to climb at a feverish pace that kept tempo with the snow that fell even harder. The snow tormented the mountain. Thick was the blizzard that pelted the leaves of the woods and filled the air with a deafening, hollow rattle. The hunter could hear nothing else. The snow blistering down upon the mountain filled his ears and blinded his eyes. His inner core was hot and wet, and yet the skin of his face was cold, even numb. And he continued to climb. And the snow continued to fall. And the sound of it falling was so complete that it was alarming to the hunter when his ears did catch another sound from someplace close by, possibly on top of the next ledge or maybe from some nearby place beyond the next tree or tree branch. The hunter marched faster, looking up the mountain from where the sound may have been and then to his left and right. He identified the sound that competed with the falling snow as a manual saw, sawing through a piece of wood. Back and forth, back and forth the sound came close to him, but it made little sense. His eyes could tell him nothing of a close presence. Up on the next ledge it must be, the sound getting louder with each step, and yet the old man did not flinch or caution his steps even though the puzzling sounds seemed to tell him that he should.

Wish …whoosh, wish …whoosh—the sound seemed to get louder and closer the faster the old man walked.

His ankles began to cramp from being flexed against the incline of the mountain for so long, but this only pushed him harder to walk faster and get to the top of the ledge. He recognized the jagged rock outcroppings and the leaning birch trees. He was halfway up the ledge. Legs grew tired and muscles began to cramp, but their master was on the move with a purpose, a mission to be accomplished up on the next ledge. And he knew as he fought the incline of the great hill with achy, tiring muscles and a sweat that grew cold and froze against his face that once on top he would have to go even farther and face the elements for even longer and still would in all probability come up short in claiming the ultimate prize of the woods. The sawing sound grew louder and a bit more pronounced until it seemed to be right in front of the old man. The sound began to change from the *wish … woosh* to a dry, sharp hiss, and the old man could feel it vibrating and ruminating under his coat.

Just before reaching the last third of the face of the ledge, he stopped and listened. The sawing and hissing sound was rumbling like the motor of a house cat stuffed under his coat, and he realized for the first time that he was in grave trouble. He was sweaty, and when he stopped on the incline to catch his breath, he felt the sweat run cold on his head and neck and felt the soapy sweat under the many thermal layers. The old man's lungs had produced the sounds he was hearing above the choir of snowfall. As he stood very still, the chaotic breathing turned into an uncontrolled heavy, wet, wheezing. He sensed the time was near. It was too late to turn back. There was no turning back. With the last bit of unexhausted energy from his legs, he thrust himself forward up the remaining half of the ledge. The wheezing grew louder and dryer as the sawing sound emanated from under his coat and exited through his mouth. On all fours, gun strap tight on his shoulder and the rifle on his back, he climbed. His hands felt the snow-covered rocks, and every crevice provided leverage that afforded him one more step. Through the trees, over the rocks, he continued on without mercy for himself. The hunter forged up the ledge using a rock outcropping as leverage to pull his stressed body the last several feet to the top. A line of spruce hung over the ledge. The old man crawled like a maimed animal to the base of one of the spruce. Using the last bit of energy, he slung the rifle off his shoulder and it fell harmlessly into the fluffy snow. He turned himself over onto his side, pushed himself up to the base of the spruce, and leaned his back up against the bark. Pulling the rifle from the snow, he rested it on his lap.

In the time it took the hunter to climb the ledge, nearly a foot of snow had fallen. The heavy limbs of the spruce kept the ground near its base free of the heaviest snow. The old man lay still. The snow fell all around him. The limbs of the spruce sheltered him. The old man closed his eyes and tried to catch his breath. The sweat ran cold on his face, but he could not feel it. His cheeks were numb. His breathing calmed and the only sound was that of the heavy, falling snow. It was a tranquil sound. Eyes closed, he drifted off with the deep sound of the falling snow. The cold could not get to him now. The rawness in his lungs no longer compromised him. The time was at hand, and he was where he wanted to be. He was drifting ever further off with the cold and the snow, but it did not matter, for the old man did not feel the cold or the raw pain in his lungs. He was at peace and lay up against the spruce in a solemn, silent state of rest. When he opened his eyes, the great buck was before him. The buck stood proud. All but cocky in appearance, the buck looked at his subject up against the tree. The hunter looked back. The rifle lay across his lap. The hand that laid across the stock, the finger that had pulled the trigger on so many occasions, was at the ready. The hunter's eyes were keen on the trophy that stood in their sights. A hunter's seasoned nerves were controlled and his heart beat hard, getting ready to skip a beat. The perfect machinery to end a morning's hunt with a decisive blow, the Marlin lay at the ready to do the job one final time.

The buck, unwavering in brute strength, was the picture of dominance and as ruler of the woods stood as such. Nostrils flaring, the king looked at the near-paralyzed subject against the tree. And the old man saw the great buck before him, an awesome presence standing as only a king could. A massive, muscular body stood profiled to the old man, but with the foremost quarters turned, facing him. The neck, thick and long, lay balanced between a pair of prime cut shoulders. The eyes big and black cast their glare into the eyes of the old man, signaling to him that this was not the first time their eyes had met. Atop the head, resting firm between its ears was the crown jewel. The rack of vanilla horns stood high off the head and swept upward and outward. Where the buck stood, no trees could conceal his seal of authenticity. The vitality of the whole species of deer was strong with this rack. There was no denying the legitimacy of this buck as the greatest genetic imprint to run Jenkins Mountain or rub its tree limbs. The old man's eyes saw and believed. He was filled with euphoria. The two stared at each other.

The hunter lifted the rifle to his shoulder. A finger gently cradled the trigger. An eye peered down the rifle's sights. The hunter's nerves told him that the experience was with him. He let out one long breath. With the next beat of his heart, it would all be over. The great buck would go down easy.

But the next heartbeat never came. The snow continued to fall. The old hunter slumped and the rifle fell. He could feel his soul drifting from his body, sliding away, his being becoming lighter even with the heavy snow pelting down on him. The whitetail gave the hunter a subtle nod before he turned and walked solemnly and gracefully away from the fallen one. In the hunter's glazed eyes, the great buck proceeded to get smaller and smaller as he walked the slow but valiant walk, until the distance and the falling snow eventually swallowed him up. The serene moment had disappeared in the snow squall, but it was followed by a euphoric if not one more angelic display.

As a mist of light pushed through the trees, the falling snow swirled in its rays. Figures moved between the trees. Silhouettes, they kicked up the snow and shook the evergreen trees. The branches rustled nervously, shaking the snow from their thick needles. The invisible became visible as the distance closed between their ghostly presence and the old man. The old man was not afraid, but rather curious as to the cause of the visions he was having. They neither seemed to linger nor move, but rather grew larger and longer in presence. The old man concentrated on the figures. He thought he heard them call to him. In faraway voices they called his name.

"El … mer, El … mer."

He looked for them. *Someone's out there. People coming through the snow, maybe to look for me. Where did they come from? Who are they?* There was a boy, ragtag-looking, walking through the trees, and then another and another. They were poorly dressed. The boys walked in single file toward the uppermost part of the mountain in the same direction as the buck, and parallel to where the old man lay. They were still far off. The old man tried to make sense of what he was seeing. He squinted his eyes and held a glove over his brow to keep the falling snow from obstructing his view. The boys looked at him with smiles, but did not walk over to help him. Instead, they called to him as if to say hello and continued on their way. And there was an older man in raggedy leggings and boots. He wore an overcoat and was followed by another and then another. They had guns, old-fashioned black powder guns. And then there were more men and more boys, and more after that, and they had horses and the horses pulled the cart wagons through the snow without the slightest stress. The old man thought he heard the men yell to him, "Elmer, come with us! Come with us!"

Their voices echoed and then were muffled by the snow and the wind. They did not stop to help him. There was no tension on their faces or urgency in their gait, even though the storm was on them and the wind ripped through them. The line of men and boys and horses and wagons grew longer. They marched in procession as an army. They marched as legends. These men and boys were the heroes of a revolution. How many times must they have retraced their steps and yet were never seen by the living who shared the mountain with them. Beyond the marching soldiers, further up on the hill, was a man on horseback reviewing the marchers as they snaked on by. He was a stately-looking man of older years and white hair. He sat erect on his horse, and his mount stood at attention under him, both of them still as a great statue. This gentleman was dressed as the impeccable soldier; cocked hat, leggings, boots, and spurs, sword about his side, and a long cape that blew only slightly with the currents of the wind. Superb in his appearance, his manner conveyed supreme strength in character and discipline. The old man recognized him but could not bring himself to utter his name. He would not need to, for in an instant the gentleman soldier far up on the hill looked at the old man and gave a brief yet impressionable nod before pulling the reigns in and spurs under his powerful mount to gallantly move amongst the river of men. The impeccable horseman rode hard up the crest of the great hill, the hooves of his powerful mount plundering through the snow, and then with a strong squall, disappeared like dust over the other side. The old man gasped. The soldiers kept walking in single file.

"Hey old man," called out one soldier, a thin, middle-aged bag of bones in rags of red and blue, "aren't you gonna come with us ghosts?"

A group of boys marching together laughed and howled into the wind of the squalling snow. One of the boys lagged behind. He was not dressed like the others. The old man recognized him. The boy called to him.

"Daddy, come on Daddy." The boy motioned with his arm. "Come Daddy, it's time. It's time for you to come, Daddy. Mommy says you're almost home. Mommy's waiting for you. She says hurry up Santa!! Hurry up!"

"My son! Can it really be my son?"

The old man was overcome with joy. He rose to his feet but left his rifle in the snow. He would need it no more. The soul of Elmer Ebenezer Schoonmacker rose and walked to his son. Together, hand in hand, father and son walked to the crest of the hill where a blinding light appeared, and the two disappeared as dust over the other side.

***

High up on the great hill of Jenkins Mountain stands the king of the mountain. He wears a crown of horns that sits tall and proud upon his head. The horns are the envy of all creatures including man, although they have but one master. Those that look to find him either for sport or respite are in awe of his awesome strength ... and they should be.

When a hunter roams the hills or climbs a mountain
ledge, or walks softly over a plot of farmland,
When he casts his sights through a meadow of birch
or sits to collect his thoughts on a rock wall,
When the autumn winds blow the leaves so red
and orange to fall upon his hunting coat,
And when the hunter breathes in the crisp,
autumn air, he will know the ground on which
he walks is sacred ground not belonging but only
for a brief time to the visitors of the woods.
And he will also know that I was once here.
When the fall comes, think of me.
I can be found on Jenkins Mountain.

Epilogue

A warm house
Fire in the woodstove
Turkey in the oven, crackling and sputtering
Homemade bread rising
The smell of warm pumpkin pie
cooling on the kitchen table
Sounds of laughter and children playing
Oh, what a joy, these times spent with family
that keep us traveling on that road
Making our way home again

Driving down that country road
Past the open field
Once green fields filled with life
That bring back days gone by
Days when we were young and spry
All those springs when we were young

The snows melt
The mountain streams flow again
They flood the brook that meanders through the field
Cold, crisp mountain air says good morning to the valley
The deer jump and play in the meadow

David Francis

The field becomes green again
The blue birds awaken it from its slumber

Driving down that country road
Past the open fields
The deer play in the distance
Oh, won't they bring back the many days gone by
Those days when we were young and spry

The post that held the fence together
Long was the fence that kept the field in place
The fence is gone, and only the fence post remains
No longer does it stand up and down, but
rather leans to the wind- blown side
The wild rose bush supports the fence post
It wraps its thorns around the weathered
post, protecting it from strangers

The field long neglected grows trees now and cedar bushes
The farmer was seen long ago traveling
down that road beside the field
But he has since not returned

CPSIA information can be obtained at www.ICGtesting.com
Printed in the USA
BVOW071652091111

275680BV00001B/47/P